SOMETHING DIFFERENT

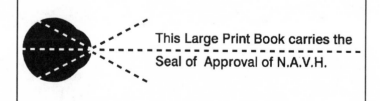

This Large Print Book carries the
Seal of Approval of N.A.V.H.

SOMETHING DIFFERENT

KAY HOOPER

THORNDIKE PRESS

A part of Gale, Cengage Learning

Detroit • New York • San Francisco • New Haven, Conn • Waterville, Maine • London

Thorndike Press® Large Print Famous Authors.
The text of this Large Print edition is unabridged.
Other aspects of the book may vary from the original edition.
Set in 16 pt. Plantin.
Printed on permanent paper.

LIBRARY OF CONGRESS CATALOGING-IN-PUBLICATION DATA

Hooper, Kay.
   Something's different ; Pepper's way / by Kay Hooper.
     p. cm. — (Thorndike Press large print famous authors)
   ISBN-13: 978-1-4104-0991-1 (alk. paper)
   ISBN-10: 1-4104-0991-0 (alk. paper)
   1. Large type books. I. Hooper, Kay. Pepper's way. II. Title. III.
Title: Pepper's way.
PS3558.O587S66 2008
813'.54—dc22
                                                 2008021800

Published in 2008 by arrangement with The Bantam Dell Publishing Group, a division of Random House, Inc.

A writer is only as good as those rare and unrewarded friends who bolster, cheer (or jeer), criticize, question, applaud — or just listen in sympathetic silence. Ideas bounce off these friends, plots are tried for effect, character motivation explored. Discussions go on over the phone; across coffee tables or dinner tables; and in the presence of baffled, bemused spouses.

And you thought I wrote alone.

Pam and Bob, this one's for you.

ONE

Gypsy hit her brakes instinctively and swerved as the small brown rabbit darted across the road in front of her car. Satisfaction and relief at not hitting the creature were short-lived, however, as a sudden and savage jolt informed her that her already battered VW had been rear-ended.

Her head snapped back and then forward, banging into the steering wheel with enough force to give her a brief view of stars in broad daylight. She found herself fighting various laws of motion in an effort to bring the car and herself safely to the side of the road. Her heart lodged in her throat for one flashing instant, because the side of the road was a narrow strip of dirt bordering on a sheer drop. And, Gypsy thought, neither she nor the car had wings.

Sputtering, the VW's engine voiced an unmistakable death rattle and expired as the little blue car with its bright yellow daisy decals lurched onto the strip of dirt. Gypsy heard a more powerful engine rumble into silence behind her. Automatically and needlessly she pulled up the emergency brake and turned off the ignition switch.

Although her forehead throbbed painfully, and the sickening fear at her near-maiden flight over the cliff hadn't quite faded, Gypsy's thoughts were crystal-clear and crazily detached.

Not again. This could *not* be happening to her again. It was the third time in six months, and poor Daisy was certainly *dead.* Judging by the sound of the impact, not even the best body-and-fender man would be able to pound the dents out. And Daisy's engine had quite definitely been mortally wounded.

Gypsy abruptly became furious at whomever had murdered poor Daisy.

The sound of the other car's door slamming was followed swiftly by a startlingly deep and coldly controlled masculine voice. "Are you all right?" it demanded, and then added icily, "Don't you know that it's illegal as well as unsafe to drive a car without brake lights?"

Gypsy fumbled for Daisy's door handle and struggled out, letting her anger at Daisy's assassin have full rein. "*You* hit *me,*

8

dammit, and Daisy *did* have a brake light —
the left one! Now you've killed her —" She
broke off abruptly as she got her first clear
look at Daisy's assassin. He didn't look like
a killer.

He was slightly under six feet tall, wide-
shouldered but slender, and finely muscled.
His burnished copper hair was thick and
slightly shaggy, a bit longer than collar
length. Eyes of an astoundingly intense
shade of jade-green shot icicles at her. But
his obvious anger couldn't hide the shrewdness behind his eyes, and the rigidly held
expression only emphasized his marvelous
bone structure.

Not a bit like a killer, Gypsy mused. . . .

Recovering from her initial surprise,
Gypsy was just about to light into the handsome stranger when he aimed the first
thrust.

"My God! I thought the last of the flower
children grew up years ago!"

She automatically looked down at herself;
there was nothing unusual. Faded, color-
fully patched jeans, a tie-dyed T-shirt,
ragged sneakers, and a silver peace sign
dangling around her neck on a leather
thong. She supposed that his description fit,
but the thrust didn't go home. In the first
place one did not normally dress neatly to

perform the errand Gypsy had just completed, and in the second place she didn't much care how she looked — and this man's distaste did nothing to change that.

She rather pointedly eyed his neat, three-piece business suit, spending a long moment gazing at extremely shiny shoes. Then she let her gaze wander briefly to the gleaming silver-gray Mercedes before returning it to his face. Satisfied with his reaction — a slight reddening beneath the tan of his cheeks — she let the matter drop, refusing to correct his first impression.

Dropping the easily assumed dignity, she spoke heatedly. "You hit Daisy from behind, and that makes it your fault!"

He sent a faintly bewildered glance toward Daisy's crumpled rear end, but said shortly, "You had no brake lights."

"Big deal!" she snapped. "If you'd been watching where you were going, you would have seen me swerve to miss that rabbit, and — Oh! Corsair!" Hastily she turned back to her car.

"Corsair?" the man muttered blankly, standing where she'd left him between their two cars and watching her open her car door and extract a bundle of cream-colored fur from inside. As she turned back toward him, he saw that the bundle was a large —

a very large — Himalayan cat. Its face, paws, and tail were a dark chocolate color, and its broad face wore what seemed to be a permanently sulky expression.

"Just look at him!" she said angrily. "It's not enough that you killed poor Daisy; you nearly gave Corsair a heart attack!"

To the man's clear, jade eyes, Corsair didn't look as though he'd ever be — or had ever been — startled by anything short of a massive earthquake. He started to make that observation out loud, then realized that by participating in this ridiculous conversation, he'd only prolong it.

"Look —" he began, but she cut him off fiercely.

"This is all your fault!"

Jade eyes narrowed in sudden suspicion. "You're certainly hell-bent to prove this was my fault, aren't you? I'll bet you don't even — How old are you?" he demanded abruptly.

Gypsy drew herself up to her full height of five nothing and deepened her glare. "You should never ask a woman her age! Where did you learn your manners?"

"Where you learned yours!" he retorted irritably.

Into that tense confrontation came a slow, grinding *thunk,* and Daisy's entire engine

11

hit the ground in a little puff of dust.

Gypsy stared rather blankly for a moment and then began to giggle. "Poor Daisy," she murmured.

The man was leaning back against the low hood of his car chuckling quietly, his icy temper apparently gone. "Why don't we start over?" he suggested wryly. "Hello, I'm Chase Mitchell."

"Gypsy Taylor," she returned solemnly.

"Gypsy? Now, why doesn't that surprise me?"

"No reason at all, I'm sure." Gypsy sighed, her amusement brief. "How am I going to get home? Daisy isn't going anywhere without the aid of a tow truck."

"I'll take you. We have to exchange insurance information anyway." He was looking down disgustedly at the slightly crumpled hood that he'd just stopped leaning against, then looked up quickly as a thought apparently occurred to him. "You *are* insured?" he asked carefully.

Knowing full well that Daisy's lack of brake lights made her at least partially to blame for the accident, Gypsy had stopped protesting. "Certainly I'm insured," she responded with dignity. After a beat she added, "At least . . . well, I think I am."

"How can you not be sure?"

"Well, I move around a lot." Unconsciously Gypsy had gravitated closer to the dented Mercedes. "Sometimes the notices from the insurance company get lost in the mail or —" She broke off hastily as she noted a disconcertingly icy storm gathering in his jade eyes. Gypsy loved a good storm, but she wasn't an idiot. "I'm insured. I know I'm insured."

"Right." As pointedly as she had done before, Chase looked from the top of her short black curls to the toes of her sneaker-clad feet. In between he noted a petite but nicely curved figure that in no way belonged to a teenager, and a face that was lovely — with fine bone structure and wide, dreamy gray eyes. "I thought you were about fifteen," he murmured almost to himself, "but I think I was wrong."

Gypsy blinked. "You certainly were." She was neither flattered nor insulted. "By about thirteen years. I'm twenty-eight." She blinked again, and added in a scolding voice, "And that was a sneaky way to find out!"

He grinned suddenly, and Gypsy was astonished at the change it wrought in his stern face. The jade eyes gleamed with amused satisfaction, laugh lines appearing at their corners, and white teeth flashed in a

13

purely charming and surprisingly boyish smile.

"Well, I had to find out," he said. Before she could ask why, he was going on briskly. "Hop in and I'll take you home."

Having always relied on her instincts about people, Gypsy didn't worry about getting into a car with a stranger. Not this stranger. For some reason she instinctively trusted him. With a sigh and a last lingering glance toward the fallen Daisy, she started around to the passenger side of the Mercedes. Then she hesitated and went back to her car long enough to pull the keys from the ignition.

"Shouldn't you lock it up?"

"Why?" Gypsy asked wryly, heading back to the Mercedes. "Daisy isn't going anywhere."

Conceding the point, he got in the driver's side of his car, shut the door, and started it up. "Where to?"

Gypsy pointed along the winding, steadily uphill road. "Thataway. Follow the yellow brick road."

As the Mercedes pulled onto the road and began to climb smoothly, Chase distinctly felt baleful eyes on him. He risked a glance sideways, and found that it was the cat's gaze he was feeling.

14

Because of a childhood allergy — and no inclination since then — he'd had little experience with cats. But he recognized the expression on this one's face. Only cats and camels could stare through supposedly superior human beings with such utter and complete disdain. It gave him a disconcertingly invisible feeling.

Caused by a cat, it was a hell of a reaction, Chase thought.

"Your cat doesn't like me," he observed, eyes firmly back on the tricky business of negotiating the road's hairpin curves.

Gypsy looked at him in surprise, and then glanced down at the cat resting calmly in her lap. Corsair was fixedly regarding one chocolate paw. "You're imagining things," she scoffed lightly. "Corsair's never met anybody he didn't like."

Chase risked another glance, and then wished he hadn't. "Uh-huh. So why is he glaring at me?"

Gypsy glanced down again. "He isn't. He's looking at his paw." Her voice was mildly impatient.

Chase decided not to look again. He also decided that Corsair was a sneaky cat. "Never mind. Tell me, Miss Taylor —"

"Gypsy," she interrupted.

"As long as you'll return the favor."

15

"Fine. I hate formality."

"Gypsy, then. Where exactly do you live? I know this road, and it dead-ends a mile or so further up. There are two houses —"

"One of them's mine," she interrupted again.

"Yours?" He sounded a bit startled.

"I'm house-sitting," she explained absently, looking out the window and thinking as she always did, that it was nice to have the Pacific for a backyard. "The owners were temporarily transferred to Europe — six months. I'll be sitting for them another four months."

"I see."

He sounded rather faint, and Gypsy looked over at him in amusement. "I'm not quite as disreputable as I look," she said gently. "I'm dressed like this because I had to take Corsair to the vet."

"And the peace sign?"

His mind obviously wasn't on the conversation, and Gypsy wondered why. "It was a gift from some friends. Sort of a private joke," she explained automatically, gazing at him searchingly. She thought that he had the look of a man who had bitten down on something and wasn't quite sure what it was. Odd. Before she could attempt to probe the cause of his strange expression —

16

Gypsy wasn't at all shy — he was speaking again.

"Do you live around here? When you're not house-sitting, I mean."

"I live wherever I happen to be house-sitting. Before this, I was in Florida for three months, and before that was New England. I like to move around."

"Obviously."

"Not *your* favorite life-style, I see," she said wryly.

"No." Abruptly, he asked, "Do you live alone?"

Gypsy thought briefly of all the bits of information a single woman generally didn't reveal to strange men — like whether she lived alone. However, if she was any judge of character, this man hardly had rape or robbery on his mind. "Usually I don't. A housekeeper usually lives with me; she's a good friend and practically raised me. But she's visiting relatives right now, so I'm on my own. Why do you ask?"

"Just wondering." He sent a sidelong glance her way. "You aren't wearing a ring, but these days asking a woman if she's single doesn't automatically preclude a live-in 'friend.' "

Gypsy looked at him thoughtfully and tried to ignore the sudden bump her heart

17

had given. She'd been on the receiving end of enough male questions to know what that one was pointing to, and it was not a direction she wanted to explore. As handsome as Chase Mitchell undoubtedly was, Gypsy nonetheless told herself firmly that she wasn't interested. At this point in her life, a man was a complication she hardly needed.

And Chase Mitchell would prove to be more of a complication than most, she decided shrewdly. They obviously had nothing in common, and he wouldn't be the sort of man who could fit in with her offbeat life-style.

Frowning, Gypsy wondered at the trend of her own thoughts. Why on earth was she hesitating? Usually she disclaimed interest immediately in order to avoid complications before they arose.

Before she could further explore her inexplicable hesitation, Chase was going on in a smooth voice.

"Of course, you could have a 'friend' who doesn't live with you." It was definitely a question, she thought.

Gypsy answered wryly, "The way I move around?"

"Some men would consider plane tickets a small price to pay," he murmured.

She wondered if that was a compliment,

but decided not to ask. With that kind of fishing she was half afraid of what she might catch. Instead, she chose a nice, safe, innocuous topic. "Do you live around here?" she asked casually.

He nodded, his eyes again on the road. The road was still both winding and tricky, but it no longer bordered on the cliffs. Trees hid the ocean now as they progressed further inland. "I've always lived on the West Coast," he said. "Apart from school years, that is."

Gypsy nodded and sought about for more safe topics. "Nice car," she finally managed inanely.

"It was," he agreed affably.

She shot him a goaded glare and immediately became more irritated when she noted that he wasn't even looking at her. "I didn't *mean* to wreck your nice car," she said with dignity. "And if it comes to that, you didn't exactly leave Daisy in great shape, you know!"

"If I were you," he suggested, ignoring the larger part of her accusation, "I'd get another car."

"Well, you're not me. I've had Daisy since I was seventeen; she's a classic. She's also my good-luck charm."

"Judging by the number of dents in her

19

that I can't claim credit for," Chase said dryly, "she doesn't seem to have been very lucky." He was completely unconscious of following Gypsy's lead in using the feminine pronoun to describe Daisy.

Uncomfortably aware of her accident-prone nature, she didn't dispute his point. And she was enormously relieved to see her house as they finally completed the long climb and the road leveled off. She pointed and Chase nodded, slowing the Mercedes for the turn into her driveway.

Her home for the next four months was a sprawling house, modern in design but not starkly so. Lots of glass, lots of cedar. It blended in nicely with the tall trees, and from the back it boasted a magnificent view of the Pacific. But the house next door was by far the more beautiful of the two. It *was* starkly modern, geometric in design, with an abundance of sharp angles and impossible curves. Cunningly wrought in glass, cedar, and stone, it was a jewel utterly perfect in its setting. And the landscaping around the house was among the most beautiful Gypsy had ever seen.

She usually didn't care too much for modern houses, but she loved that one. Glancing toward it as the Mercedes pulled into her driveway, she wondered for the hundredth time who lived there. She'd only seen a gardener who came every day to care for the trees and shrubs.

The thought slipped from her mind as Chase stopped his car just outside the garage. Reaching for the door handle, she said, "You'd better come in; it may take a while for me to find the insurance card."

He nodded and turned off the engine, his eyes fixed curiously on the somewhat battered trailer pulled over onto the grass beside the driveway. "What —" he began.

Gypsy slid from the car before explaining. "That," she told him cheerfully, "contains all my worldly possessions when I move. Aside from Corsair, that is; he rides in Daisy with me." She reflected for a moment as she watched Chase move around to her. "Although I don't suppose one could call a cat a possession."

"Not any cat I've ever heard of," Chase agreed, eyeing Corsair with disfavor. "They seem to be complete unto themselves." He accompanied Gypsy and friend up the walkway.

She fished her keys from a pocket and unlocked the heavy front door. Opening it and stepping inside, she murmured, "I suppose I should warn you."

"Warn me? About wha—" Beginning to

follow her inside, Chase suddenly found himself pinned solidly against the doorjamb by two huge paws. Inches from his nose loomed a black and white face in which a grin of sorts displayed an impressive set of dental equipment. It was a Great Dane, and it looked as though it would have considered half a steer to be a tidy mouthful.

A calm Gypsy holding an equally calm Corsair studied Chase's still face for a long moment. "Meet Bucephalus," she invited politely. "He was named after Alexander the Great's horse."

"Obviously," Chase murmured carefully. "Two questions. Is it yours?"

"No; he belongs to the Robbins couple — the ones who live here. Second question?"

"Does he bite?"

"No." She considered briefly. "Except for people who rear-end cars. He makes an exception for them."

"Funny lady. Would you mind getting him down?"

"Down, Bucephalus."

The big dog immediately dropped to all fours, looking no less huge but considerably more friendly. His long tail waved happily and he tilted his chin up slightly in order to wash Corsair's face with a tongue the size of a hand towel. The cat suffered this indignity with flattened ears and silence.

Chase carefully shut the door, keeping a wary eye on the dog. "Any more surprises?" he asked ruefully.

"I shouldn't think so. This way." She led him down the short carpeted hallway. A huge sunken den at the end of the hall boasted a brick fireplace, a beamed ceiling, and an open *L*-shaped staircase leading up to a loft. The furniture consisted of an off-white pit grouping with abundant cushions, a large projection television, and assorted tables and lamps.

Gypsy stepped down into the den, set Corsair on the deep-pile carpet, and immediately headed for a corner that was either an afterthought to the beautiful room, someone's idea of humor . . . or both.

Chase followed slowly, staring in astonishment. The corner was partitioned off from the room by an eight-foot-tall bookcase, clearly made from odd pieces of lumber and sagging decidedly in every shelf. It was crammed to capacity. Within the "room" was a battered desk that had seen more mileage than Daisy; it was cluttered with papers, a couple of dog-eared dictionaries, stacks of carbon paper, and a few more unidentifiable items. A ten-year-old manual typewriter sat squarely in the middle of the clutter.

"Your corner," Chase murmured finally.

"My corner," Gypsy confirmed absently, scrabbling through a desk drawer.

Chase wandered over to examine the bookshelf, uneasily aware that the giant Bucephalus was right beside him. Trying to ignore his escort, he scanned the titles of Gypsy's books, becoming more and more puzzled. "I've never seen so many books on crime and criminology in my life. Don't tell me you're also a cop?"

Still searching for the elusive insurance card, Gypsy answered vaguely, "No. Murder." She looked up a moment later to find him staring at her with a peculiar expression, and elaborated dryly, "Murder *mysteries. I write murder mysteries."

"*You? Murder mysteries?"

"I wouldn't laugh if I were you. I know ninety-eight ways to kill someone, and all of them are painful."

Chase absorbed that for a moment. "Do your victims lose their insurance cards?" he asked gravely.

"My victims are usually dead, so it doesn't matter. Damn. It's not here."

Chase was frowning. Then the frown abruptly cleared and he was staring at her

24

in astonishment. "No wonder your name rang a bell! I've read some of your books."

"Did you enjoy them?" she asked him politely.

"They were brilliant," he replied slowly, still staring at her in surprise. "I couldn't put them down."

Accustomed to the astonished reaction to her authorship, Gypsy smiled faintly and began to search through the clutter on her desk. "Don't bother telling me that I don't look like a writer," she advised. "I've heard it many times. I'd like to know what a writer is supposed to look like," she added in a reflective voice.

Chase discovered that he had been absently petting Bucephalus and stopped, only to continue hastily when the dog growled deep in his throat. "Can't you tell this monster to lie down somewhere?"

"Tell him yourself. He knows the command."

"Lie down," Chase said experimentally, and was immediately rewarded when the dog flopped down obediently. Stepping carefully around Bucephalus, Chase approached Gypsy and observed her unfruitful search. "Can't find it?"

Gypsy lifted a feather duster and peered beneath it. "It's here somewhere," she said irritably. "It has to be."

"You could offer me a cup of coffee while I wait," he said reproachfully.

"It isn't Tuesday."

Chase thought that one over for a moment. No matter how many times he ran it through his mind, her meaning didn't appear. "Is that supposed to make sense?"

She looked up from her search long enough to note his puzzled expression. "I only fix coffee on Tuesday," she explained.

"Why?" he asked blankly.

"It's a long story."

"Please. This is one answer I have to hear."

Gypsy pulled a squeaky swivel chair out and sat down, beginning to search through the center drawer for a second time. "When I was little," she told him patiently, "I became addicted to iced tea. My mother thought that it was unhealthy, that I needed to drink other things like milk. I hate milk," she added parenthetically.

"So anyway Mother decided to assign different drinks to the days of the week. That way, she could be sure that I was getting a healthy variety. By the time I got around to drinking coffee, the only day left for it was Tuesday. And today isn't Tuesday."

Chase shook his head bemusedly. "When you adopt a habit, it's your life, isn't it?"

"I suppose."

"Well, what's today's drink?" he asked, deciding to go with the tide.

"Is today Friday? Let's see. . . . Friday is wine. Or a reasonable facsimile thereof." She looked up with sudden mischief in her eyes. "Mother doesn't know about that. Poppy — my father — told me that I'd better save Friday for when I grew up. So I did. It's a good thing I listened to him. I like wine."

Staring at her in fascination, Chase murmured, "You seem to have . . . interesting parents."

"To say the least." Abruptly she asked, "What do you do for a living?"

Chase blinked, but quickly recovered. "I sell shoes," he replied blandly.

With sudden and disconcerting shrewdness, she said calmly, "If you're a salesman, I'll eat my next manuscript — page by page."

Chase wondered why he'd lied, then decided that it had probably been due to sheer bewilderment. "I'm an architect."

Gypsy made no comment on the lie, other than a brief look of amusement. "Now, *that* I believe. Residential or commercial?"

"Commercial. I've designed a few private homes though."

"Would you like some wine?" she asked suddenly.

After a moment Chase complained, "You take more conversational shortcuts than any person I've ever met."

"It saves time," she said solemnly.

He decided again to go with the tide. By this time he was beginning to feel like a piece of driftwood being battered against the shore. "Yes, I'd like some wine. Thank you."

Gypsy frowned. "I'd better see if I have any." She rose from the chair and headed for the hallway, saying over her shoulder, "Go through the desk again, will you? I may have missed it."

It took Chase several seconds to realize that she meant the insurance card. With a shrug he sat down in the creaky chair and began searching through the desk.

He'd searched three drawers by the time Gypsy came back into the room carrying two glasses filled with white wine. "Find it?" she asked, handing him a glass.

"No. Tell me something." He waved a hand at the general clutter of her desk. "How can someone so obviously disorganized write such ruthlessly logical and neatly plotted books?"

"Luck, I guess."

Chase lifted an eyebrow at her as she rested a hip against the corner of the desk. "Luck. Right." He lifted his glass in a faint toast, but the expression on his face indicated that he was not toasting Gypsy's answer but rather some wry thought of his own.

"Tell you what." He sighed almost to himself. "Why don't you keep looking for the card? Maybe you'll have found it by the time I pick you up tonight."

"Pick me up? For what?"

"Dinner."

TWO

"Dinner?" Gypsy leaned an elbow on her typewriter and stared at Chase. The reluctance in his voice had been so audible as to be ludicrous, and she fought an urge to giggle. "You don't really want to do that."

"No," he agreed amiably. After a moment he added cryptically, "I've always considered myself an intelligent man."

Was that supposed to make sense? she wondered. "Look, if you're feeling guilty because of what you did to Daisy —" she began, but he cut her off decisively.

"I'm not feeling guilty about Daisy; the accident was more your fault than mine. And taking women out to dinner because I feel guilty isn't one of my noble habits. Do you want to go or don't you?"

Gypsy sipped her wine to give herself time to think. After hesitating, she asked cautiously, "Why are you asking me?"

He stared at her. "You want to hear my

motives, I take it?"

"A girl likes to know where she stands."

"Well, my motives are the usual ones, I suppose. Companionship. Interest in a lovely woman. A dislike of eating alone. And," he added wryly, "I think that I should get to know my next-door neighbor."

Gypsy blinked. "You live . . . ?" She gestured slightly and sighed when he nodded. "You've been gone for two months."

Chase nodded again. "Back East working on a project."

"You didn't know Bucephalus," she pointed out.

"I hardly knew the Robbins couple. And I never saw that dog before today. They must have kept him hidden, although how to hide something that big . . . Are you going out with me?"

Gypsy hesitated again, and somewhere in the back of her mind her uncertainty was still nagging her. "Chase. . . ." She was searching for the right words. "If you want a companion across the dinner table, that's fine. If you want a neighbor you can borrow a cup of sugar from, that's fine. Anything more than that isn't fine. I don't want to get involved."

"I see." Chase set his wineglass on top of a dictionary, then took hers from her hand

31

and set it down also. "That's an interesting point."

"What is?" she asked blankly.

"Whether we could become involved with each other. Would Bucephalus protect you?"

Gypsy had the detached feeling that there was something here she was missing totally. Deciding that the simplest course would be to answer his question, she said, "I suppose he would. If I screamed or something."

"Don't scream." Chase rose to his feet and pulled her upright into his arms.

"What're you . . . ?" she sputtered, caught off guard.

"A little experiment," he murmured. "To see if we could become involved with each other." Before she could utter another word, his lips had unerringly found hers.

In that first instant Gypsy knew that she was in trouble. Definite trouble. A fiery tingle began in her middle and spread rapidly outward to the tips of her fingers and toes. It was totally unexpected and frighteningly seductive. And Gypsy couldn't seem to find a weapon to combat the stinging little fire.

Something had kicked her in the stomach; dizziness overwhelmed her, and shock sapped the strength from her knees. Her body seemed to disconnect itself from her mind, her arms lifting of their own volition to encircle his neck. She felt her lips part beneath the increasing pressure of his, and then even her mind was lost. Searing brands moved against her back, pulling her body inexorably against his, and the hollow ache in her middle responded instantly to the fierce desire she could feel in him.

Gypsy was aware of the hazy certainty that she should stop this. Yes. Stop it, she thought. But she couldn't even find the strength to open her eyes, realizing only then that they were closed.

Stop it. In a moment. . . .

The stinging little fire wasn't so little anymore. It was a writhing thing now, scorching nerve endings and boiling the blood in her veins. She could feel her heart pound with all the wild unreason of a captive beast, and it terrified her with its savage rhythm.

She was dimly aware of drawing a shuddering breath when Chase finally released her. Her hands fell limply to her sides and then reached back to clutch at the edge of the desk she was leaning weakly against. Wood. Solid wood, she assured herself. Reality.

She stared at him with stunned, disbelieving eyes, only partially aware that his breathing was as ragged as hers and that the jade eyes held the same expression of bemused shock as her own.

Chase lifted his wineglass and drained it very scientifically. "Scratch one casual friendship," he muttered hoarsely.

Gypsy immediately shook her head. "Oh, no," she began.

"I've been wanting to do that," he interrupted musingly, "ever since you told me about coffee on Tuesday."

She blinked and then fiercely gathered her scattered wits. "No, Chase," she said flatly. "No involvement."

"Too late."

Hanging on to the desk as if to a lifeline, she shook her head silently, ignoring the sneering little voice inside her head that was agreeing with his comment.

"I don't know about you, but I'm not strong enough to fight," he said wryly.

Gypsy silently ordered the little voice to shut up and took hold of her willpower with both hands. "No involvement," she repeated slowly.

He gazed at her with a disconcerting speculation. "I'm reasonably sure it isn't me," he observed, "so what is it?"

For the first time her small work area was giving Gypsy a claustrophobic feeling, and she pushed away from the desk to wander out into the den. She sat down rather bonelessly on a handy chair and watched as Chase followed her into the main part of the room. Since he had a somewhat determined expression on his face, she searched hastily for words.

"Gypsy —"

"Chase, I — Oh, hell." She decided on honesty. "Chase, I've never . . . slept with a man before."

"You haven't?" Something unreadable flickered in his eyes.

"No."

"Why?"

She bit back a giggle, her sense of humor abruptly easing the tension in her body. "A girl used to have to explain why she did; now she has to explain why she doesn't."

"The times they are a changin'," he murmured.

"Uh-huh." She gave him a wry look. "Look, I've spent most of my life traveling, which isn't exactly conducive to lasting relationships. Summer flings and one-night stands hold no appeal for me. It's got nothing to do with morality, it's just me. In spite of my footloose life-style, I'm the home and hearth type at heart."

"A ring and a promise?"

Gypsy shook her head patiently. "That's just it: I don't want to get married."

Chase sank down in a chair across from hers and peered at her bemusedly. "You've just done an about-face here, haven't you?"

"Not at all. I'm trying to make a point. The only relationship acceptable to me would be a lasting relationship with one man — which, to my mind, means marriage. But at this point in my life I don't want to get married. So . . . no relationship."

"No involvement," he murmured.

Gypsy felt an enormous sense of relief when he seemed to understand. She also felt oddly disappointed. The resulting confusion left her unusually nervous. What on earth was wrong with her? She had a book to write, and heaven knew that would occupy her for weeks. Why this sudden wish that she had not voiced her "no involvement" policy. Policy? That made her sound like a politician!

"You never gave me an answer."

"What?" She stared at him, trying in vain to read his expression. "Dinner? I . . . can't. I have a deadline, and I need to organize my notes and get to work."

"You have to eat."

"Yes, well. . . ." She produced a weak smile

from somewhere. "If you'll take a close look at my typewriter, you'll probably find crumbs inside. I usually eat right over the keyboard."

"You'll get ulcers eating like that," he warned dryly.

Gypsy shrugged and murmured vaguely, "Deadlines, you know." She hoped that she'd given him the impression her deadline was considerably closer than it actually was. Little white lies never hurt anyone, she reasoned and, besides, she needed time to figure out what was wrong with her.

Along those lines she abruptly changed the subject. "Did you design your house?"

Chase didn't even blink; apparently he was getting accustomed to her conversational leaps. "Yes. Like it?"

"It's beautiful. I've never seen anything like it. Did you design it especially for yourself, or did you just decide afterward that it was for you?"

"It was mine all the way. Shall we talk of cabbages and kings now?" he added politely, doing a bit of conversational leaping of his own.

Gypsy sighed. It was not, she reflected, going to be easy for her to hold her own with this man. He seemed to be extremely adaptable. As unusual as she obviously was

37

in his experience, he had learned quickly how *not* to be thrown off balance by her. "I don't know what you mean."

"You know. Can you cook?" he asked abruptly.

He was using her own tactics on her, damn him! Gypsy sighed again and mentally threw up her hands in surrender. For the time being, at least. "No, I can't cook. Also I can't sew, and I hate washing dishes." If she'd hoped to discourage him with these admissions of unfemininity, she was defeated.

"Nobody's perfect. What's your favorite meal?"

"Spaghetti."

"My speciality. What time would you like to eat?"

Gypsy decided that either the wine, the kiss, or both had addled her wits; otherwise she'd be a lot sharper than she seemed to be at the moment. Was he or wasn't he riding roughshod over all her objections? "I'm working, I told you."

"You have to eat. I'll do the cooking. My place or yours?"

With some vague idea of having the home-team advantage, she said, "Mine. Can you really cook?" She was suddenly dimly astonished to realize that she'd just *let* him ride roughshod over all her objections.

"They teach you to at military schools," he answered absently, his mind obviously on something else.

"You went to military schools?"

"Grew up in them." Gypsy had his full attention now. "My father hoped I'd go on to West Point, but I had other plans."

She'd had little experience with father-son relationships, but she was apparently the type of person that others invariably confided in, so she'd heard many tragic stories resulting from conflicts over career choices. Chase certainly didn't look to be the victim of a tragedy, but her ready sympathy was nonetheless stirred.

"Was he . . . very upset?" she probed delicately.

"He wasn't happy," Chase replied wryly. "I told him I was getting even for all those lonely years spent in military schools."

"Oh, poor little boy!" she said involuntarily. To her surprise Chase flushed slightly. But there was a considering expression in his jade eyes.

"If I were an unscrupulous man, I'd take advantage of your obvious sympathy," he told her gravely. "However, since the last thing I want to do is to begin our . . . friendship with a lie, I'll confess that my child-

39

hood wasn't in the least deprived."

"It wasn't?"

"Hell, no." He smiled at her. "The schools were good ones, I had plenty of friends, and Dad visited frequently. He always came and whisked me away to whatever post he happened to be at for holidays and vacations. I was a seasoned world traveler by the age of twelve."

Gypsy had to admit that it didn't sound sad, but she was still puzzled. Chase calmly enlightened her.

"My mother died when I was five, and Dad couldn't very well drag me all over the world with him. More often than not, he was assigned a post squarely in the middle of some revolution. So I went to boarding schools, where I learned to pick up my socks and cook spaghetti. Good enough?"

She nodded slowly. "Sorry to be nosy."

"Not at all. I'm glad you're interested. It'll be my turn to hear your life story tonight." He held up a hand when she would have spoken. "Fair trade. And I *have* to hear more about your parents. What time shall we have dinner?"

She stared at his politely inquiring face for a long moment. "About seven. I guess," she added rather hastily, deciding that she was giving in too damn quickly.

"Fine. I'll come over around six and bring the fixings with me." He rose to his feet and made a slight gesture when she would have got up. "Don't bother. I think I can find the door. See you at six. Oh, and keep looking for that insurance card, will you?"

Gypsy gazed after him, and she felt a sudden pang. Not a pang of uneasiness or uncertainty, but one of sheer panic.

I don't know about you, but I'm not strong enough to fight.

Reluctantly she allowed her mind to relive that . . . kiss. Kiss? God! Vesuvius erupting had nothing on that "kiss," Gypsy thought. She had never in her life been shaken like that. And Chase had made no secret of the fact that it had shaken him as well.

And that meant trouble with a capital everything.

She rubbed absently at the sudden gooseflesh on her arms, wondering at the inexplicable caprices of fate. Her life was going so smoothly! And she didn't want the status quo to change . . . not now. Her writing produced enough upheaval for any sane person; asking for more was like asking for a ringside seat at the hurricane of the century.

By the time Chase knocked on her door at

41

six on the dot, Gypsy had come no nearer to an answer. She'd had several hours to think and in all that time, her thoughts had turned continually to that kiss.

She knew that her peculiar life-style and offbeat habits had caused her to miss a lot. She had friends, but not close ones. During high school and college, she'd indulged in the normal sexual experimentation, but a natural unconformity had kept her safe from peer pressure. And she hadn't cared for any man enough to attempt the serious relationship that her own private ideals demanded.

But she had convinced herself over the years that the only things she had missed by her celibacy had been vulnerability and potential heartache. And she knew from experience that it demanded a rare and extremely adaptable person to survive — happily — living with her. To date only Amy, her housekeeper and mother hen, had managed the feat.

Not even her loving and uncritical parents, unusual themselves, had been able to live with their daughter once she'd reached adulthood. And if *they* couldn't do it, what chance had the sane, normal man? Gypsy wondered.

So when she opened the door to let Chase in at six, she was staunchly determined to nip any romantic overtures in the bud. After which, according to all the books on etiquette, the noble warrior would retire from the field in dignified defeat.

The problem was . . . Chase apparently intended to retire from the field only if carried off on his shield.

"Did you find it?" he asked cheerfully.

Belatedly shutting the door behind him and hurrying down the hall to keep up with his tall form, Gypsy struggled briefly to figure out what he was talking about. "The insurance card? Yes, I found it." She followed him into the modern kitchen, reflecting absently that he looked *really* good in jeans. "It was in Corsair's envelope."

"Corsair's what?" He paused in unloading a bulging grocery bag onto the deep orange countertop, looking at her blankly.

Gypsy was staring at his T-shirt and trying not to giggle. Obviously he wasn't as conservative as she'd first thought. The T-shirt read: THIS IS A MOVING VIOLATION. Above the words was a picture of a leering man chasing an obviously delighted and sketchily dressed woman.

Trying to keep her voice steady, Gypsy finally replied to his question. "Corsair's envelope. You know, where I keep his vet

43

records."

"Oh. I won't ask what it was doing there." He went back to unloading the groceries.

"Uh . . ." She gestured slightly. "Nice shirt."

"Thank you. Is it too subtle, do you think?"

"Depends."

"On what?" He looked at her with innocent mischief in his eyes.

"On whether it's a declaration of intent."

"Bite your tongue." He looked wounded. "I would never be so crass."

Gypsy wasn't about to ask what the shirt was if it *wasn't* a declaration of intent. She decided to leave the question of subtlety up in the air for the time being.

Chase was looking her up and down, considering. "You look very nice," he commented, eyeing her neat jeans and short-sleeved knit top. "But what's this?" he asked, reaching out to pluck a pair of dark-rimmed glasses from the top of her head.

"They're working glasses." She reclaimed them and placed them back on top of her head. "To help prevent eyestrain, according to the doctor."

"Oh." Chase removed the glasses from the top of her head and placed them on her nose. He studied the effect for a moment while she frowned at him, then said, "They make you look very professorial."

She pushed them back up and said briefly, "They make me look like an owl. If you want me to help cook, by the way, the consequences will rest on your head."

Chase accepted the abrupt change of subject without a blink. "You get to watch the master chef at work. Sit on that stool over there."

Gypsy debated about whether or not to dig in her heels. "Those military schools didn't help your personality," she offered finally in a deceptively mild voice.

"I take it you dislike being ordered around."

"Bingo."

"Will you *please* sit on that stool, Miss Taylor, so that I can demonstrate my culinary skill before your discerning eye?"

"Better," she approved, going over to sit on the high stool.

"Trying to reform a man is the first sign of possessiveness, you know." He was unloading the bag again.

"I've taught *manners* to quite a few children," she responded politely, refusing to be drawn.

"Really? How did that come about?" Chase was busily locating what he needed in cabinets and drawers. "I assumed you didn't have any siblings."

"You assumed correctly." Gypsy reflected wryly that he had a disconcerting habit of dangling a line her way and then abruptly cutting bait when she ignored it. "But I like kids, so I usually find a nursery school or kindergarten wherever I'm living and volunteer to help out a couple of days a week."

"So you like kids, eh?" He sent a speculative glance at her as he began to place hamburger in a pan for browning. "I'll bet you'd eventually like to have a houseful of your own."

"You'd lose the bet. I'd make a lousy mother; I'm not planning on having kids at all."

Chase halted his preparations long enough to give her a surprised look. "Why do you think you'd make a lousy mother? Your 'gypsy' life-style?"

She shook her head. "I grew up that way, and it didn't bother me. No, it's my writing. Some authors work nine to five with nights and weekends off, just like an average job." She smiled wryly. "And then there's me. When I'm working, it's usually in twelve- to fourteen-hour stretches. For weeks at a time. I lose pounds and sleep . . . and sometimes friends. I swear and throw

46

things and pace the floor. Corsair, poor baby, has to remind me to feed him." Her smile unconsciously turned a bit wistful. "What kind of life would that be for kids?"

Chase was watching her with an expression that was curiously still. After a moment he shook his head as if to throw off a disturbing thought. When he spoke, it was about her work habits, and not about her decision not to have children. "Aren't you afraid of burning yourself out?"

"Not really." She spoke soberly. "Notice that I said *when* I'm working. I usually take a break of several weeks between books. I'm healthy and happy — so where's the harm?"

He shook his head again — this time in obvious impatience. "You need someone to take care of you."

"I *have* someone to take care of me — my housekeeper, Amy. The hamburger's burning."

Turning swiftly back to the stove, Chase swore softly. He repaired the results of his inattention silently, then said, "Tell me about your parents. Your mother first; I have to hear about the creator of coffee on Tuesday."

"You're hung up on that." Gypsy sighed. "Well, Mother is an artist — very vague, very creative. She's also a spotless housekeeper, which drives both Poppy and me absolutely nuts; he and I share an extremely untidy nature." She sought about in her mind for a further description of her mother. "Mother is . . . Mother. She's hard to describe."

"An artist? Would I have heard of her?"

"Know anything about art?"

"Yes."

"Then you've heard of her. Rebecca Thorn."

Chase nearly got his thumb with the knife he was chopping onions with. "Good Lord! Of course I've heard of her." Staring at Gypsy, he nearly got his forefinger with the knife. "You come from a very illustrious family."

"You haven't heard the half of it."

"Your father too?"

"Uh-huh. You'd have to be a scientist to recognize his name though. He's a physicist. Disappears periodically and can't talk about his work." She reflected for a moment. "Poppy looks like the typical absentminded professor. He's soft-spoken, very distin- guished, and wouldn't pick up a sock if it were made of solid gold."

She grinned suddenly. "It's amazing that he and Mother have lived together in perfect harmony for nearly thirty years. If I didn't know the story behind it, I'd wonder how Poppy ever managed to catch Mother."

"What *is* the story?"

"Never mind."

"Unfair! It'll drive me crazy."

"Sorry, but it's not my story. If they come over to visit, you can ask. They live in Portland."

"I thought they traveled?"

"Used to. Poppy still has to fly off somewhere occasionally, and Mother has her showings from time to time, but they're pretty settled now."

Cutting up ingredients for a salad, Chase glanced at her innocently. "They're so different, yet they get along perfectly?"

Gypsy missed the point. "Usually. Although they told me that there was a definite disagreement before I was born. Mother decided to go on tour when she was six months pregnant, and Poppy protested violently. You'd have to know Poppy to realize how astonishing that is. He never gets mad."

"What happened?"

"Well, Poppy said that he'd be damned if he'd have his child born in an elevator or the back room of some gallery — quite likely, given Mother's vagueness — and that she wasn't going to exhaust herself by trying to give showings in twelve cities in twelve days, or something equally ridiculous. So he planned a long, leisurely tour lasting three months and went with her, and the government was having kittens."

Chase blinked, digested the information for a moment, and then asked the obvious question. "Why?"

"Why was the government having kittens?" Gypsy looked vague. "Dunno exactly. Poppy was working on something for them, and they got very cranky when he took a sudden vacation. They couldn't do much about it, really, since genius doesn't punch a time-clock."

After staring at her for a moment, Chase asked politely, "And where were you born?"

She looked surprised. "In Phoenix. Mother woke up in the middle of the night having labor pains. She got up and called a cab; she knew that she wouldn't be able to wake Poppy — he sleeps like the dead — so she went on to the hospital alone. The problem was, she forgot to leave poor Poppy a note. He nearly had a heart attack when he woke up hours later and found her gone."

Chase had a fascinated expression on his face. "I see. So you were born in a hospital. Somehow that seems an anticlimax."

"Actually I was born in the cab. They

made it to the hospital, and the cabbie ran inside to get a doctor. The doctor got back to the cab just in time to catch me. The cabbie — his name is Max — still sends me birthday cards every year."

Chase leaned back against the counter, crossed his arms over his chest, and shook his bowed head slowly. It took Gypsy a full minute to realize that he was laughing silently.

"What's so funny?"

He ignored the question. "Gypsy," he said unsteadily, "I have *got* to meet your parents."

Puzzled, she said, "They'll be here on Sunday for a visit; you can come over then." She had totally forgotten her intention of discouraging Chase's interest.

"Thanks, I'll do that." Still shaking his head, he went back to fixing the salad. A moment later he softly exclaimed, "Will you look at that?"

"What?" She slid off the stool and went over to peer around him.

"Your knife bit me." Chase quickly held his right hand over the sink, and a single drop of blood dripped from his index finger to splash onto the gleaming white porcelain. "Or the Robbinses' knife. Whichever —"
He broke off abruptly as a muffled thump

51

sounded behind him.

Gypsy opened her eyes to the vague realization that she was lying on the coolness of a tile floor. A pair of jade eyes, concerned, more than a little anxious, swam into view. She gazed up into them dreamily, wondering what she was doing on the floor and why Chase was supporting her head and shoulders. He looked terribly upset, she thought, and didn't understand why the thought warmed her oddly.

Then her memory abruptly threw itself into gear, and she closed her eyes with the swiftness born of past experience. "I hope you put a Band-Aid on it," she said huskily.

"I have a paper towel wrapped around it," he responded, a curious tremor in his deep voice. "Gypsy, why didn't you tell me you couldn't stand the sight of blood? God knows I wouldn't have thought it, considering the type of books you write."

"It's not something I normally announce to everybody and his grandmother," she said wryly, opening her eyes again. "Uh . . . I think I can get up now." She felt strangely reluctant to move, and grimly put that down to her sudden faint.

"Are you sure?" Chase didn't seem to be in any great hurry to release her. "Did you hit your head when you fell?"

"If I did, it obviously didn't hurt me. Help me up, will you, please?" She kept her voice carefully neutral.

Silently he did as she asked, steadying her with a hand on each shoulder until the last of the dizziness had passed. "Are you sure you're all right?"

"I'm fine." Gypsy made a production out of straightening her knit top. "Sorry if I startled you."

"*Startled* me?" Chase bit off each word with something just short of violence. "You scared the hell out of me. How on earth can you write such gory books when you can't stand the sight of blood?"

Patiently Gypsy replied, "I don't have to *see* the blood when I write — just the word."

He stared down at her for a long moment, shaking his head, until the bubbling sauce on the stove demanded his attention. He was still shaking his head when he turned away. "I hope you don't have any more surprises like that in store for me," he murmured. "I'd like to live to see forty."

Curious, Gypsy thought, then shrugged. Turning away, she caught sight of Corsair. The way he was sitting by one of the lower cabinets communicated dramatically. She frowned slightly as she got his cat food out and filled the empty bowl at his feet. "Sorry, cat," she murmured.

"What about Bucephalus?" Chase asked, obviously having observed the little scene.

"I fed him earlier."

"Oh." Leaping conversationally again, he said, "Tell me something. Why is it that the heroes in your books really aren't heroes at all? I mean, half the time, they're nearly as bad as the villains."

"Heroes don't exist," she told him flatly, going back to sit on her stool.

He tipped his head to one side and regarded her quizzically. "You're the last person in the world I'd expect to say something like that. Care to explain what you mean?"

"Just what I said. Heroes don't exist. Not the kind that people used to look up to and admire. The heroes available today are the ones created years ago out of pure fantasy."

"For instance?"

"You know. The larger-than-life heroes who were always fighting for truth, justice, and the American way. Superman. Zorro. The cowboys or marshalls in the white hats. A few swashbucklers. Knights on white chargers. They're all fiction . . . or just plain fantasy."

Chase set the bowl filled with tossed salad into the nearly barren refrigerator. "No modern-day heroes, huh?"

"Not that kind, no. The larger-than-life heroes are either long dead or else buried in the pages of fiction. It's a pity, too, because the world could use a few heroes."

Spreading French bread with garlic butter, Chase lifted a brow at her. "Those words carry the ring of disillusion," he said. "Don't tell me you're a romantic at heart."

Gypsy squirmed inwardly, but not outwardly. "I know that's a sin these days."

"No wonder you haven't gotten involved with anyone."

"You're twisting my meaning," she said impatiently. "I would never expect any man to measure up to fantasy heroes. That's as stupid as it is unreasonable. But there's a happy medium, you know. It's just that . . . romance is gone. I don't mean romance as in love or courtship. I mean *romance.* Adventure, ideals."

She ran a hand through her black curls and tried to sum up her meaning briefly, feeling somehow that it was important for him to understand what she meant. "Fighting for something *worth* fighting for."

Chase was silent for a long moment, his hands moving surely, and his eyes fixed on them. Then he looked over at Gypsy, and the jade eyes held a curiously shuttered expression. "Heroes."

"Heroes." She nodded. "Now, master chef — when do we eat?"

THREE

Thinking back on it the next day, Gypsy had to admit — however reluctantly — that Chase was a marvelous companion. He'd kept her interested and amused for several hours, telling her all about what it was like to grow up in military schools — one prank after another, judging by some of the stunts he and friends had pulled — and how clients could easily drive an architect crazy.

And he asked questions. About the different places she'd lived, about her parents, about how she wrote her books. He plied her with an excellent red wine, pressed her to eat more spaghetti than Italy could have held, and then refused her virtuous offer of help in cleaning up the kitchen.

He left on the stroke of midnight . . . with a casual handshake and a cheerful goodbye.

Not *quite* what Gypsy had expected.

Rising on Saturday after an unusually restless night, she fiercely put him out of her mind. She fixed herself a bowl of cereal for breakfast, absently noting that she was nearly out of milk. She fed Bucephalus and Corsair, unlatched the huge pet door leading from the kitchen out into the backyard, and rinsed her cereal bowl.

Saturday was juice, so she carried a large glassful out to her desk. Orange juice today; she usually alternated between orange, grape, or tomato juice. Wearing a pair of cutoff jeans and a bright green T-shirt, she sat down at her desk to work.

Two hours later Gypsy discovered that she'd been shuffling papers around on her desk, and had accomplished absolutely nothing.

Physical labor — that's what she needed. Working at a desk was fine, but working at a desk meant thinking, and she was thinking too damn much about Chase Mitchell.

Locating her gardening basket with some difficulty — why was it in the bathroom? — she went out into the front yard. There were several flower beds all bearing evidence that she'd indulged in physical labor quite often during the last two months.

Gypsy was a good gardener. And she had not merely the proverbial green thumb but a green *body*. Flowers that weren't even supposed to be blooming this time of year were waving colorful blossoms in the early-morning breeze. The half-dozen flower beds in the front yard were beautiful.

She glanced around, remembered where she'd left off, then dropped to her knees beside a flower bed ringing a large oak tree at the corner near Chase's property. She attacked a murderous weed energetically.

There was a sudden rustle in the tree above her, and then a metallic sound as a bunch of keys fell practically in her lap. Gypsy stared at them for a long moment. Keys. *Not* acorns. She looked up slowly.

Chase was lying along a sturdy-looking lower limb, staring down at her. He was dressed casually in jeans and a green shirt, open at the throat, and the only way to describe his expression would be "hot and bothered."

"What are you doing?" she asked with admirable calm.

"Getting my car keys," he replied affably.

"Oh, is that where you keep them?"

"Only since I met your cat."

Gypsy's gaze followed his pointing finger and located Corsair, who was sitting farther out on the same limb. The cat's furry face was a study in innocence, and his bushy tail was waving gently from side to side.

Gypsy looked back at Chase in mute inquiry.

Chase crossed his hands over the limb and rested his chin on them, with all the air of a man making himself comfortable. "Your cat," he explained, "has somehow found a way into my house. Beats me where it is, but he's found it. He was sitting on my couch a little while ago — with my car keys in his mouth. I chased him three times around the living room and then lost him. The next thing I knew, he was sitting outside the window, on the sill. When I came out of the house, he climbed this tree. Ergo, I climbed up after him."

"Uh-huh." Gypsy glanced again at the innocent cat. "Why would Corsair steal your keys?"

"You don't believe me?"

"Forgive me. I've known Corsair a little longer."

"He stole my keys."

"Why would he do that?"

"How the hell should I know? Maybe he wanted to drive the car; God knows, he's arrogant enough."

"Don't insult Corsair, or I won't let you climb my tree anymore."

"Cute. That's cute."

"Chase, cats don't steal keys. And Corsair's never stolen anything." Gypsy exercised all her willpower to keep her amusement buried. She waved the trowel about. "What would he want with your keys?"

"He wanted to annoy me. I tell you, that cat doesn't like me!"

"Well, if you keep on calling him *that cat* in that tone of voice, I wouldn't be surprised if he actually did start disliking you. Besides, it's obvious that you know nothing about cats. *If* he disliked you, he'd shred your curtains or attack you when you weren't looking, or something like that. *Not* steal your keys."

"He stole my keys."

Gypsy stared up into stubborn jade eyes. "Of *course*, he did. He just sat down and decided very logically that since he didn't like you, he'd steal your car keys. Then he'd let you chase him three times around your living room. Then he'd let you chase him up a tree —"

"All right, all right!" Chase sighed in defeat. "Obviously I imagined the whole thing."

"Obviously." Gypsy went back to work with the trowel.

There were several rustling noises from above. Then a muffled "Damn!" Then a long silence. Gypsy kept working; another weed poked up an unwary head and she attacked it lethally.

"Want to give me a hand here?"

Gypsy murdered another weed. "A grown man can't get down from a tree by himself?" She had to swallow hard before the question would emerge without a hint of the laughter bubbling up inside of her.

"I'm not too proud to ask for help." There was a pause. "Help!"

She sat back on her heels and looked up at him. She was trying desperately to keep a straight face. "What do you want me to do? Climb up and get you down, or cushion your fall?"

There was a frantic gleam in the jade eyes. "Either way — when I get down. I'm going to murder you!"

"In that case, stay where you are."

"Gypsy —"

"All *right!* What's the problem?"

"I can't look over my shoulder to see where to place my feet. Every time I try, I lose my balance. And stop grinning, you little witch!"

"I'm not grinning. This isn't grinning." Gypsy struggled to wipe away the grin. "It's a twitch. I was born with it."

"Sure. Tell me where to put my feet."

Gypsy swallowed the instinctive quip.

"Uh . . . slide back a little. Now a little to the right. No, *your* right! Now . . ."

A few moments later Chase was safely on the ground. Gypsy, who hadn't moved from her kneeling position, looked up at him innocently. "That'll teach you to climb trees. What would you have done if I hadn't been here?"

"Perished in agony. I thought you were supposed to be working."

"I told you I worked odd hours."

"What're you doing now?"

"What does it look like? I'm planting weeds."

"You have a sharp tongue, Gypsy mine."

She ignored the possessive addition to her name. "One of my many faults." She tossed him the keys. "Don't let me keep you," she added politely.

Deliberately misunderstanding her, he asked solemnly, "Would you keep me in comfort and security for the rest of my life? I have no objections to becoming a kept man."

The unexpected play on words knocked her off balance for a moment — but only for a moment. She and her father had played word games too many times for this one to throw her. "I won't be a keeper; the pay's not good enough."

63

"But there are benefits. Three square meals a day and a place to rest your weary head." He sat down cross-legged on the grass beside her, still grave.

"Not interested."

"A live-in proofreader."

"I can read."

"Typist?"

"I'll ignore that." Gypsy weeded industriously.

"That's not a weed," he observed, watching her. The word game was obviously over for the moment.

"It is too. It's just pretending to be a flower."

"What are you pretending to be?"

"A gardener. If you're not leaving, help weed."

"Yes, ma'am." Chase searched through the wicker garden basket, obviously in search of a tool with which to weed. "Why is there a dictionary in this basket?"

"Where do *you* keep dictionaries?"

"One would think I'd learn not to ask you reasonable questions."

"One would think."

"Do you do it deliberately?"

Gypsy gave him an innocent look. "Do what deliberately?"

"Uh-huh." He sighed. "There's a fork

64

here; shall I use it to weed?"

"Be my guest."

"Would you like to have lunch?" he asked, using the fork enthusiastically to destroy a marigold in the prime of life.

Gypsy gently removed the fork from his grasp. "Not just after breakfast, no."

"Funny."

"Sorry." She hastily took the fork away from him a second time. "No more help, please. I don't want Mr. and Mrs. Robbins to come home to a bare lawn."

"Are you criticizing my gardening skills?" he asked, offended.

"Yes."

"Oh."

"No wonder you hire a gardener."

"You made your point. I didn't rub it in that I cook better than you."

"Not better. You cook — I don't. Period."

"Whatever." Chase sighed and got to his feet. "Well, since you won't let me weed, I'll be on my way. Do you need anything from town? I have to run some errands."

Gypsy paused in her work long enough to look up at him. "Now that you mention it — I could use a gallon of milk."

"Is Saturday milk day?" he asked interestedly.

"No, Monday is."

65

"You're going to drink a gallon of milk on Monday? It'll spoil if you don't."

"I use it for cereal. That doesn't count as a drink."

"Right." He nodded slowly. "Uh . . . what're you doing this afternoon?"

Glancing past his shoulder, Gypsy saw Corsair about to launch himself. "Step back!" she ordered briskly.

Instinctively Chase did so, and Corsair overshot him to land with a disgruntled expression in the grass beside Gypsy. The cat's face seemed to proclaim irritably that not even a cat could pause to correct his aim in midair.

"I told you he didn't like me."

Gypsy swatted the cat firmly. "Leave!"

Corsair stalked toward the house with offended dignity.

"Sorry," Gypsy murmured. "I can't understand it; Corsair likes everybody."

"Everybody but me."

"I may have misjudged you about the keys," Gypsy said slowly.

"Good of you to admit it."

"I'm nothing if not fair."

"I won't comment on that. You didn't answer my question. What're you going to be doing this afternoon?"

"I usually go for a walk on the beach, but

66

I won't know for sure what I'll be doing until then."

"Don't believe in planning ahead, eh?"

"I treasure spontaneity."

"I'll keep that in mind. One gallon of milk coming up." Lifting one hand in a small salute, Chase headed across to his house.

Gypsy stared after him. It occurred to her that anyone listening to one of their conversations — particularly if he or she came in on the middle of it — would be totally bewildered. Neither she nor Chase ever lost the thread. It was as if they were mentally attuned, on the same wavelength.

It was a disturbing thought.

She put more energy into her attack on the weeds, slaughtering without mercy while frowning at the thoughts that flitted through her mind.

She was in trouble. *Definite* trouble. Chase possessed a sharp intelligence, a highly-developed sense of the ridiculous, and an indefinable talent for holding her interest — no mean accomplishment, considering her wayward mind. He was also fatally charming.

Besides . . . she'd always had a thing about redheads.

Gypsy uprooted a marigold by mistake, and hastily replanted it. Damn! She was

67

thinking about him too much. It didn't help to remind herself of that. Long hours at her typewriter had taught her that the mind was a peculiar instrument, given to absurd flights of fancy all mixed up with spans of rational thought.

If only there were a lever that she could switch from ABSURD to RATIONAL. But no such luck.

Her lever was stuck on ABSURD. Or something was. Why else was she kneeling here on the grass and wistfully contemplating a relationship with a man? Particularly *that* man?

"Face it," she told four marigolds and a rose. "You'd drive him crazy inside a week — once you really started to work. And he'd play merry hell with your concentration."

She worked vigorously with the trowel to loosen the soil around her audience. "And you don't want to get involved. You *don't.* Just think . . . you'd have to live in one house for *years.* And he'd expect you to learn how to cook — you know he would. And he wouldn't like whatisits in the refrigerator, or dirty clothes strewn through the house, or cat hair on the couch. Especially Corsair's hair.

"The smart thing to do would be to sink

68

your scruples and settle for an affair," she told her audience, dirt flying like rain as she unconsciously dug a hole at the edge of the bed. "At least then you wouldn't have to go to court whenever he decided that enough was enough. You'd just politely help him pack his suitcases — or pack yours — and call it quits. Nice and civilized."

She frowned as a drop of moisture fell onto her hand. "Oh, for Pete's sake," she muttered angrily, swiping at a second tear with the back of one dirty hand. "It hasn't even *begun,* and already you're crying because it's over!"

Gypsy filled the minor excavation with dirt, dropped the trowel into her basket, and rose to her feet. She picked up the basket and stared down at the colorful flowers for a moment. Then she turned and made her way toward the house.

"Everybody talks to plants," she muttered aloud. "They make good listeners; they don't butt in with sensible suggestions, and they don't warn you when you're about to make an utter fool of yourself!"

Since Chase had arranged to have Daisy towed to a garage for repairs (Gypsy didn't hold out much hope), she was pretty much housebound. Chase hadn't specified any length of time for his "errands," but the morning dragged on with no sign of him, and Gypsy was bored.

She didn't feel like writing. Gardening had palled decidedly. She played fetch with Bucephalus for an hour, but then *he* got bored. She tried to teach Corsair to play the same game; for her pains, she got a stony glare from china-blue eyes and a swishing tail indicative of cold contempt.

"Why do I put up with you, cat?"

"Waurrr."

"Right. Go away."

She watched as Corsair headed for the shade of a nearby tree in the backyard, then glanced at her watch. Twelve o'clock. The morning was gone, and she hadn't accomplished a thing. Wonderful.

Gypsy walked across the lawn to the redwood railing placed about two feet inside the edge of the cliff. She leaned on the railing for a few moments, gazing out over the Pacific and thinking muddled thoughts. Maybe a walk on the beach would clear the cobwebs away.

She followed the railing to the zigzagging staircase leading down to the beach. On the way down, she absently glanced across to the twin staircase leading from Chase's backyard. The beach below was narrow as beaches go, but it was private for a quarter of a mile in either direction. North and south of the private stretch were various small towns, and, of course, other privately owned properties.

But only these two homes possessed the eagle's perch of the cliffs. In this area anyway.

Gypsy loved it.

Barefoot as usual, she walked out to the water's edge and stood listening to the roar of the surf. It was a comforting sound. A *comfortable* sound. Endlessly steady, endlessly consistent, though at the moment it possessed the disturbing trick of reminding one of one's own mortality.

Frowning, Gypsy turned and walked back a few feet toward the cliffs. She stopped at the large, water-smoothed rock jutting up out of the sand. It was a favorite "place of contemplation" for her, and she sat now in the small seatlike depression in its side.

Mortality.

It was one of those odd, off-center, out-of-sync moments. Gypsy wasn't generally given to soul-searching, but in that moment she searched. And she discovered one of life's truths: that complacency had a disconcerting habit of shattering suddenly and without warning.

How many times had she told herself that her life was perfect, that she had no need to change it? How many times had she asserted with utter confidence that she needed no one but herself to be happy?

Gypsy's frown, holding a hint of panic, deepened as she stared out over the ocean. Had she been wrong all these years? No. No, not wrong. Not *then.* She'd needed those years to work at her writing, to grow as a person.

But had she grown? Yes . . . and no. She'd certainly grown as a writer. And she was a well-rounded person; she had interests other than writing, and she got along well with other people. But she'd never opened herself up totally to another person.

For *person,* she thought wryly, read *man.* No relationships, other than the strictly casual. No vulnerability on that level. No chance of heartache. And . . . no growth?

She was more confused than ever. Who, she wondered despairingly, had conceived the unwritten rulebook on human relationships? Who had decreed long ago in some primal age that total growth as a human being was possible only by risking total vulnerability?

Reluctantly Gypsy turned from the philosophical and abstract to the concrete and specific. Chase.

She was reasonably certain that she didn't *need* Chase — or any other man — to be happy. At the same time she had no idea whether or not that mythical man could make her *happier.*

And for her — more so, she thought, than with most other women — any relationship would be a great risk. She already had one strike against her: She was difficult, if not impossible, to live with. And she wasn't even sure that she could live for more than a few months in one place.

And then there was —

Gypsy's thoughts broke off abruptly as a sound intruded on her consciousness. If she didn't know better . . . it sounded like hoofbeats. She got to her feet and stepped away from the rock, looking first to the south. Nope — nothing there. Definite hoofbeats, and they were getting louder. She turned toward the north.

The horse was coming up the middle of the narrow beach at a gallop. It was pure white and absolutely gorgeous. The black saddle and bridle stood out starkly, and the metal studs decorating the saddle glinted in the sunlight. And on the horse's back was a man.

In the brief moment granted her for

73

reflection, Gypsy felt distinctly odd. It was as if she'd stepped into the pages of fiction . . . or into the world of film fantasy.

The rider was dressed all in white — pants, boots, gloves, and shirt. The shirt was the pirate-type, full sleeves caught in tight cuffs at the wrist and unbuttoned halfway down. And the rider wore a mask and a black kerchief affair which hid all his hair. Almost all. A copper gleam showed.

Gypsy took all that in in the space of seconds. And then horse and rider were beside her, and the totally unexpected happened. Gypsy would have sworn that it couldn't be done except by trained stunt-people on a movie set. Forever afterward, she maintained that it was sheer luck, *not* careful planning, that brought it off.

The horse slid to a halt with beautiful precision, leaving the rider exactly abreast of Gypsy. Then the animal stood like a stone while the rider leaned over and down.

"Wha—" was all she managed to utter.

She was swept up with one strong arm, and ended up sitting across the rider's lap. Through the slits of his mask, darkened eyes gleamed with a hint of green for just a moment. And then he was kissing her.

Ravishment would have been in keeping with the image, she supposed dimly, but the rider didn't use an ounce of force. He didn't have to. He kissed her as if she were a cherished, treasured thing, and Gypsy would have been less than human — and less of a woman — to resist that.

She felt the silk beneath her fingers as her hands came to rest naturally — one touching his chest and the other gripping his upper arm. The dark gold hair at the opening of the shirt teased her thumb, and the hand at her waist burned oddly. The hard thighs beneath her were a potent seduction.

She felt the world spinning away, and released it gladly. Her lips parted, allowing — inviting — his exploring tongue. Fire raced through her veins and scorched her nerve endings. She felt the arm around her waist tighten, and then . . . the devastating kiss ended as abruptly as it had begun.

Gypsy was lowered back to the sand, green eyes glinted at her briefly, and then the horse leaped away.

Dazedly she stared after them. She took a couple of steps back and found her seat by touch alone, sinking down weakly. The horse and rider had disappeared. Without conscious thought she murmured, "Say, who was that masked man?"

Then she giggled. The giggle exploded into laughter a split second later. Gypsy laughed until her sides ached. Finally she wiped streaming eyes, and tried to gather her scattered wits. In a long and eventful life nothing quite so wild had ever happened to her.

A gleam from the sand at her feet caught her attention, and she bent down to see what it was. She held the object in her hand for a long moment, then her fingers closed around it and she laughed again.

Delighted laughter.

It occurred to Gypsy as she climbed the stairs to her backyard a few minutes later that Chase had somehow found the time to plan that little scene very carefully. Where had he got the horse? And how could he have been certain that she'd take a walk on the beach? The only thing she *didn't* wonder about was the point of it all.

Heroes.

She crossed the yard and entered the house through the kitchen, still giggling. Who would have thought the man would go to such absurd lengths to catch her attention? Why in heaven's name hadn't some woman latched onto him years ago?

Gypsy hastily brushed that last thought away.

There was a gallon of milk in her refrigerator, and no sign of the Mercedes next door. She smiled and went on through the house to her work area. After a moment's deliberation she placed the masked rider's souvenir on the middle shelf of her bookcase. She studied the effect for a moment, nodded to herself, and sat down at the desk.

This time she did accomplish some work. Her notes fell into place naturally, and she didn't foresee any major problem with the forthcoming book. Aside from pushing Corsair off the desk twice and firmly putting Bucephalus outside after he'd chewed on her ankle for the third time, she worked undisturbed.

"You should lock your doors. Anybody could come in."

It was Chase, back in his jeans and shirt of the morning, and carrying a bag from a hamburger place in town. Before she could say a word, he was going on cheerfully.

"Hamburgers; I didn't feel like cooking. Let's eat." He headed for the kitchen.

Gypsy rose from the desk, smiling to herself. So he was going to play innocent, eh? Well, she could play that game as well. It occurred to her wryly that Chase was rapidly on his way to becoming a fixture around the place . . . but she didn't have the heart to send him away.

77

At least that's what she told herself.

"How do you know I haven't already eaten?" she asked, following him into the kitchen. "It's past two o'clock."

"You've obviously been busy; I guessed that you'd forget about lunch. What's the drink for the day? I forgot to ask this morning."

"Juice. I'm having tomato."

"With hamburgers?"

"With anything. What would you like?"

"The same; I'm always open to new experiences."

Gypsy started to comment on his remark, then thought better of it. She poured the juice while he was setting out their lunch on the bar.

"Will you do something about this dog? I'm going to fall over him and break my neck."

"He's supposed to be outside. Why did you let him back in?"

"I don't argue with a dog that size."

"Right. Out, Bucephalus." She put the dog back out in the yard.

"Salt?" he asked politely, holding up a salt-shaker when they were seated.

"No, thank you." Gypsy tasted the hamburger thoughtfully. "I notice you ordered them both with everything."

"Certainly I did. That way, no one gets offended later."

"Later?"

"When we make mad passionate love together, of course."

"Is that what we're going to do?"

"Eventually."

"Oh."

"You could sound a little more enthusiastic," he reproved gravely.

"Sorry. It's just that I've never heard something like that announced quite so calmly. Or so arbitrarily."

"My military upbringing, I suppose."

"Better learn to rise above it."

"What?"

"Your military upbringing. We've agreed that I don't like to be ordered around."

"I didn't order you around. I just stated a fact."

"That we're going to make mad passionate love together."

"That's right."

"Best laid schemes, and all that."

"Ever hear the one about the dropping of water on stone?"

"Are you trying to say —"

"I'll wear down your resistance eventually."

"I wouldn't be so sure, if I were you."

"But you're not me, Gypsy mine."

"I'm not *yours* either."

"We'll be each other's — how's that?"

"The last thing I need in my life is a man who accuses my cat of leading him up a tree."

"Let's forget about that, shall we?"

"Put down that catsup bottle!" Gypsy giggled in spite of herself. "I'll never forget. That's another of my faults, by the way."

"You seem to have a regular catalog of faults."

"Precisely. Sorry for the disappointment, but I'm sure you can find somebody else to while away your vacation with."

"One of *my* faults, Gypsy mine, is that once I set my mind on something, I never give up."

FOUR

Gypsy thought about that calm statement during the remainder of the day. As a declaration of intent, she decided, it lacked something. And what it lacked was a simple *definition* of intent. Just exactly what had he set his mind on? Her, apparently. But what exactly did he —

Oh, never mind! she told herself irritably. It wasn't going to do her a bit of good to keep wondering about it.

And in the meantime Chase was making his presence felt. Not in a big way; he left right after lunch, politely saying that he didn't want to interrupt her work. But he came back. He came back four times to be precise — between three and six p.m. Each time, he stuck his head around the corner of her work area and apologized solemnly for bothering her. And each time he asked to borrow something. A cup of sugar, a stick of butter, two cups of milk, and a bud vase, respectively.

It was the bud vase that piqued Gypsy's curiosity.

"What's he up to, Herman?" she asked her typewriter after Chase had vanished for the fourth time. Herman didn't deign to reply. Herman did, however, repeat a word three times. At least she *blamed* Herman for the mistake.

She was still glowering at Herman ten minutes later, when Chase returned. He came over to the desk this time, decisively removed the sheet of paper from Herman, and then looked down at Gypsy with a theatrical leer.

"Are you coming willingly, or will I be forced to kidnap you?"

"Coming where?" she asked blankly.

"Into my parlor, of course. My house, if you want to be formal."

"Why should I come to your house?"

"You're invited to dinner."

"Invited or commanded to attend?"

"Invited. Forcefully."

"And if I politely refuse?"

"I'll throw you over my shoulder and kidnap you. Of course, if I'm forced to those lengths, no telling when I'll release you. Much better if you come of your own free will." His voice was grave.

Gypsy sighed mournfully, unable to resist the nonsense. "I suppose I'd better come willingly, then. Do I have your word of honor as a gentleman that I can come home whenever I want?"

He placed a hand on his chest and bowed with a certain flair. "My word of honor as a gentleman."

Since he was still leering, Gypsy looked at him suspiciously, but rose to her feet. "Is this a dress-up party, or come-as-you-are?"

"Definitely come-as-you-are. We'll have a dress-up party later. Better put some shoes on though."

Gypsy silently found some sandals. Corsair was sleeping on one of them and wasn't happy at the disturbance, but she ignored the feline mutters of discontent. Chase was waiting for her in the hall.

He led her out the front door and across the expanse of green lawn to his house. Since the two properties were separated by only a low hedge, broken in several places, it was a short walk. He opened one of the double doors and ushered her inside.

It was Gypsy's first look inside the house that she had admired so much from the outside. Immediately and wholeheartedly she fell in love with it.

The front doors opened into a huge, open

area. The sunken room was carpeted in a deep rust-colored pile, and both the light-colored paneling and the open, beamed ceiling added to the spaciousness. The furniture — a pit grouping and various tables — was modern. There were plump cushions in a deep ivory color, and colorful throw pillows for a pleasant contrast. A combination bookshelf and entertainment center ran along one wall, containing innumerable books, an extensive stereo system, and a large-screen television set.

If the remainder of the house looked like this . . . Gypsy took a deep breath, dimly aware of Chase's gaze on her. "Did you do the decorating?" she asked finally.

"All the way. Would you like the nickel tour?"

"Please."

The remainder of the house looked *better.* There were three bedrooms, two baths, a large study, a formal dining room in an Oriental motif, a combination kitchen and breakfast nook that Julia Child would have killed for, and a Jacuzzi.

The Jacuzzi occupied a place in half of the redwood deck in back, which stretched from the glass doors opening into the breakfast nook to the identical glass doors opening into the master bedroom. The deck was enclosed by glass around the Jacuzzi, and houseplants abounded, giving the illusion of a jungle scene.

Gypsy stared around her for a moment and sought for a safe topic. "I thought you weren't good with plants," she managed finally.

"I'm not. But for some reason, houseplants do well for me. This concludes the nickel tour, ma'am. Now, if you'll come back to the dining room with me, dinner will be served."

She preceded him silently, speaking only when they'd reached the dining room. Gazing at the table laid out formally and intimately for two, she murmured, "Now I know why you wanted the bud vase."

Chase seated her ceremoniously and in grand silence, then disappeared into the kitchen.

Gypsy stared after him for a moment, then looked back at the bud vase. After a moment she reached out and gently touched the single peach blossom it contained. Idly she wondered why he'd chosen that particular flower. Did it have some special meaning? She didn't know.

What she *did* know was that, like a person going down for the third time in a deep river, there was little hope of saving her now.

Gypsy had never in her life had pheasant under glass, vichyssoise, or anything else Chase served her that night. She enjoyed it all, but the picture they must have presented sitting at the formal table wearing jeans and casual tops caused her to giggle from time to time.

Or maybe the giggles were caused by Chase's "juice surprise."

"What is this?"

"Juice, I told you. Different kinds."

"Chase, there's more in this than juice."

"So I stretched a point a little. So what?"

"You're disrupting the habit of a lifetime, that's so what."

"It's time to broaden your horizons."

"You sound like a travel ad."

"Sorry."

"This is very good, you know."

"I'm glad you like it. It's —"

"No, don't tell me what it is," she warned hastily.

"Why not?"

"Because if it's snails, I don't want to know about it."

"It isn't snails."

"Good. Don't tell me what it *is.*"

"Whatever madam desires. Would madam like more — uh — juice?"

"Chase, are you trying to get me drunk?"

He looked scandalized. "How you could ever suspect —"

"Easily," she interrupted, peering at him owlishly.

"A *baby* has more kick than this stuff," he maintained staunchly.

"Strong baby. Shall I sit here in royal detachment while you clear the table? I'll help if you like, but I hope your china's insured."

"You stay put. I'll clear the table and bring in dessert." He began to do so efficiently.

"What's for dessert?"

"Baked Alaska."

"I'll take a wild guess," she said drily, "that you're a gourmet cook."

"Something like that."

"So tell me, master chef, to what do I owe the honor?"

"Honor?" He placed a delicious-looking dessert in front of her.

"Of having you cook for me."

"I'm trying to seduce you, of course."

Gypsy was vaguely glad that she'd swallowed the first bite before he answered her question. Otherwise, she'd have choked. "I see." She touched her napkin delicately to her lips — mainly to hide the fact that they were twitching. "The way to a woman's heart, and all that?"

Very seriously he responded, "Well, I thought that either the food would get you . . . or the juice would."

She stared at his deadpan expression. How *could* the man look so ridiculously serious? After a moment she began eating again. "I'll say this for you — the approach is certainly original. I don't think I've ever heard the brutal truth used to such good effect."

"Not *brutal!*" he protested, wounded.

She gave him a look.

Chase sighed sadly. "It isn't working, is it?"

"No." She didn't mince words. She also didn't tell him just how well his strategy was working. His straightforward approach was certainly startling, novel in her experience, and if she didn't get out of his house very quickly, she was going to make a total fool of herself.

"Aren't you tired of a predictable life?" he asked persuasively. "Wouldn't you like change, excitement, adventure?"

"Sounds like you're inviting me on a safari," she observed, eyes firmly on her dessert.

Chase gave up — for the moment, at least.

Dessert was finished in silence, and then he sent her into the living room with her juice. Gypsy didn't protest, and she didn't try to leave. The juice was beginning to have the inevitable effect on her.

But the inevitable effect on Gypsy was a bit different from what Chase had probably hoped for. Except that she didn't believe Chase had hoped for seduction at all. She had the definite feeling that he'd wanted to keep her off-balance more than anything else. However, visions of seduction or whatever notwithstanding, Chase would probably get more than he bargained for.

The juice really didn't have much of a kick. But then . . . it didn't take much for Gypsy. It didn't take much, that is, to release the reckless mischief she normally kept tightly reined.

She was going to teach him a lession, Gypsy decided.

When Chase came into the living room after clearing up in the kitchen, Gypsy was prowling the room like a caged tigress. The empty juice glass had been placed neatly in the center of the chrome and glass coffee table.

"Gypsy?"

She whirled around and flung herself into his arms. "I thought you said that we were

89

going to make mad passionate love together?" she questioned throatily, gazing up
into startled jade eyes.

Chase had automatically caught her, and
now stared down at her as though he'd
caught a bundle of dynamite with a lighted
fuse. "I did say that, didn't I?" he mumbled.

"Yes. So what are we waiting for?"

"Sobriety," he answered involuntarily.

Gypsy fiercely disentangled herself and
stepped back, regaining her balance by
sheer luck. "Did you or did you not intend
to get me drunk and take advantage of me?"
she demanded accusingly.

"Yes — no! Dammit, don't put words in
my mouth!"

"You're rejecting me!" she announced in
a hurt tone, doing a sudden and bewilder-
ing about-face.

"*No,* I'm not rejecting you! Gypsy —"

"Don't . . . you . . . touch . . . me!" she
warned awfully when he stepped toward
her. "You had your chance, buster, and you
blew it!"

For a long moment Chase looked about
as bewildered as a man could look. Then
the bewilderment slowly cleared, and a
whimsical expression replaced it. "Do you
like playing with fire, Gypsy mine?"

Damn, but he's quick! she thought wryly.

90

Deciding that there was no graceful way out of the situation, she merely shrugged with a faint smile.

"I could read a great deal into that shrug," he told her.

"Don't imagine things. Thank you for the excellent dinner, master chef, and I think I'd better be going now."

"You're welcome, and I'll walk you to your door."

His easy acceptance bothered Gypsy for some reason. It might have had something to do with the unexplained gleam in his jade eyes. Or it might have had something to do with the fact that he'd twice announced his intention of attempting to seduce her today — and no attempt had yet been made.

The walk across to her front door was accomplished in silence, with Gypsy growing more nervous with every step. Along with the nervousness was a sudden, heart-pounding awareness of the man at her side, and she realized dimly that every muscle in her body was tense.

It was neither dark nor light outside; it was that odd twilight hour. Daylight was colors, darkness was stark black and white, but twilight was elusive shades of gray.

When they reached the front porch, Chase caught her arm and turned her to face him.

Gypsy looked up at him instinctively, wary and uneasy. Her heart had recaptured its captive-beast rhythm, and she felt suddenly adrift in a dangerous and unpredictable sea.

"May I kiss you good night?" he asked softly, his hands coming to rest on her shoulders.

Gypsy wanted to say no, sharply and without mincing words. But she wasn't very surprised to find herself nodding silently.

His hands lifted to cup her face, his head bending until their lips touched with the lightness of a sigh. There was no pressure, no demand. Just warmth and sweetness, and a gentleness that was incredibly moving.

Gypsy felt herself relaxing, felt her body mold itself bonelessly to his. Her arms moved of their own volition to slide around his waist even as she became aware of his hands moving slowly down her back.

If this was seduction, she thought dimly, then why on earth was she fighting it? It was a drugging, insidious thing, sapping her willpower and causing her to forget why she should have been protesting.

A tremor like the soft flutter of a butterfly's wings began somewhere deep inside her body. It spread outward slowly, growing in strength, until she felt that her whole body was shaking with it.

When Chase finally drew away, Gypsy had the disturbing impression that she had lost something. She didn't know what it was. But the tremor was still there, and she was having trouble breathing.

The man was a warlock, she thought.

"Good night, Gypsy mine," he murmured huskily, reaching over to open the door for her.

Gypsy forced her arms to release him. "Good night," she managed weakly, sliding past him to enter the house. She hesitated for a moment, glancing back over her shoulder at him, then softly closed the door.

She went into the den and sat down on the couch, curling up in one corner and staring at the blank television screen. For a long time she sat without moving. Corsair came to sit beside her, his rough purr like the rumble of a small engine. Gypsy stroked him absently. Bucephalus came and lay down on the carpet by the couch.

Gypsy smiled wryly. "What are you two trying to do — comfort me?" she asked. A canine tail thumped the floor, and feline eyes blinked at her. "Thanks, guys, but I think it's beyond your power."

She sat for a while longer, listening to silence and the whispering voices of reason. But it was the gentle murmurs of desire that tormented her. She finally got up and went to take a long hot bath, hoping that the steam would carry away her problems.

It didn't.

She let Corsair and Bucephalus outside for a few minutes, then called them back in and latched the pet door. She wandered around downstairs for a while, until disgust with her own restlessness drove her to bed. It was midnight by the time she crawled between the sheets, and Gypsy lay there for a while and stared at the ceiling. She finally reached and turned out the lamp on her nightstand, absently moving Corsair off her foot and patting Bucephalus where he lay beside the bed.

Ten minutes later the phone rang. She picked up the receiver without bothering to turn the lamp back on, wondering who could be calling her at that hour. "Hello?"

"Will you dream about me tonight?" a deep, muffled masculine voice asked softly.

Gypsy's first impulse was to hang up. The last thing she needed tonight was a semi-obscene phone caller. But something about that voice nagged at her. It *could* be Chase, she decided finally. Besides, who *else* could it possibly be? So why not play along?

"Of course, I will," she murmured seductively.

"Sweet dreams?"

"As sweet as honey."

"I could make them even sweeter," he drawled.

"Promises, promises."

"Just give me the chance."

"A man should always . . . make his own opportunities."

"And what should a woman do?"

"She waits."

"An old-fashioned lady, I see."

"In . . . some ways." Gypsy was thoroughly enjoying the suggestive conversation.

He chuckled softly. "Sweet dreams . . ."

Gypsy listened bemusedly to the dial tone for a moment, then cradled the receiver gently. " 'Curiouser and curiouser,' " she murmured to herself. She smiled into the darkness for a while.

Then she fell asleep.

Gypsy slept six hours — no more, no less. It was a peculiarly exact habit in a quite definitely inexact person. But apparently her biological clock was set for precisely six hours of sleep and not a second more. And during those six hours, Armageddon could have occurred without disturbing Gypsy.

She dressed and went through her morning routine. She fed the animals and herself, unlatched the pet door, and checked the weather (rainy). Sunday was "dealer's choice" when it came to the day's drink. She decided on iced tea and made a pitcherful.

Since her parents were coming to visit, she unlocked the front door — heaven only knew what she'd be doing by the time they arrived, so they usually just walked right in.

Then she carried a glass of tea to her desk, put a sheet of paper into Herman, and got down to work.

The morning advanced steadily as she worked. The rain stopped and the sun came out. Her canine and feline companions checked on progress from time to time and then disappeared. Gypsy refilled her glass once.

With utter concentration and not a little willpower, she'd managed to put Chase out of her mind while she worked. And she was glad about that; not even friendship would be possible between them if thoughts of him disrupted her work, and Gypsy knew it. As impossible as she was to live with while she was writing, she was even worse when something prevented her from writing.

Around ten a.m. she heard the sound of a car in her driveway, but continued to work without a pause. If it was her parents, they'd come inside; anyone else would knock.

A few moments later her father came in. He was a tall man, slender and distinguished. His hair was black, save for wings of silver framing his lean face. Mild blue eyes gazed peacefully out from beneath straight brows. And lines of struggle coexisted peacefully with lines of humor on his face.

An interesting face for any artist — and Gypsy's mother had painted it more than once.

Gypsy lifted an absent cheek for his kiss. "Hi, Poppy," she said vaguely.

"Hello, darling." Her father saluted the cheek, and then rested his hip against the corner of her desk. Conversationally he added, "There's a man up a tree in your front yard."

"Oh?" She briskly corrected a misspelled word. "That's Chase."

"An admirer, darling?"

"Neighbor." Gypsy finished a paragraph and briefly debated over the next one before beginning to type again. "Did you ask him why he was in the tree?"

"I didn't want to pry," her sire murmured.

Gypsy acknowledged the gentle remark with a faint twinkle as she pulled the completed page from Herman. "I suppose

97

Corsair stole his car keys again," she explained cheerfully.

Allen Taylor didn't even blink. "When did Corsair start stealing keys?"

"Yesterday. Where's Mother?"

"Helping Chase, I assume. She went to see if he needed help."

"Oh. Half a minute, Poppy; let me finish this page and I'll be through for the day." Gypsy was trying desperately not to think about Chase's first meeting with her mother. But . . . oh, she wished she could be a butterfly poised on a flower out there. . . .

Just as she was pulling the last sheet out of Herman, her father spoke again. He'd wandered over to her bookcase, and now held the masked rider's souvenir in his hand.

"What's this?"

"What does it look like? It's a silver bullet obviously."

"Silver plated," her father corrected gravely.

"It's the thought that counts," Gypsy reproved.

"Oh. Where did you get it?"

"That's obvious too."

"I see." He placed the souvenir back on the shelf.

Gypsy's father was very good at not asking nosy questions.

They had just stepped into the living room when her mother and Chase came inside. And Chase looked so utterly bemused and fascinated that Gypsy wanted to burst out laughing.

Many mothers and daughters look like sisters; Gypsy and her mother looked like twins. The same height, roughly the same weight, the same short black curls and wide gray eyes. They were even dressed similarly in jeans and blue knit pullovers. It was an odd thing, but even if they were in different parts of the country, nine times out of ten Gypsy and her mother would wear at least the same colors on any given day.

Rebecca Taylor, née Thorn, looked eighteen. The only thing that set her apart from her daughter in looks was a single silver curl at her left temple. Her voice was different, slower and richer with age, but her conversation made Gypsy's sound positively rational by comparison. And she never missed a thing.

"Hi, Mother." Gypsy hugged her mother briefly. "I see you've met Chase."

"Yes. Gypsy, you need to talk to Corsair. Stealing keys is a very irritating habit."

"I will, Mother." Gypsy swallowed a laugh

99

as she glanced at Chase. "Poppy — Chase Mitchell. Chase, my father, Allen Taylor."

Still bemused, Chase nearly forgot to shake hands.

It was a fun day. Gypsy's parents had the knack of setting anyone at ease immediately, and they both obviously liked Chase. As for Chase, he'd apparently decided to go with the tide. Although he still tended to blink whenever he looked at Rebecca — particularly whenever she and Gypsy were standing near each other — he was quickly back on balance again.

Rebecca commandeered the kitchen to cook lunch, towing Chase along behind her when Gypsy helpfully mentioned his culinary skill. Allen and Gypsy were almost immediately ordered to make a trip to the store when the cupboard was found to be bare. Corsair and Bucephalus got into the act, mainly by being constantly chased from the kitchen by Rebecca.

When Gypsy looked back on the day, she remembered snippets of conversations, frozen stills from the action.

"Why didn't you tell me that your mother was also your twin? I made a total fool of myself in that tree!"

"There are no fools in my mother's orbit — just interesting people."

"I wish I could believe that."

"Believe it. My mother *expects* to find strange men in trees."

"A sane man would run like a thief in the night."

"Are you sane?"

"Apparently not."

"He's a redhead."

"Yes, Mother."

"Temper?"

"So far, no. But give him time; I only met him Friday."

"I like his eyes. Would he sit for me?"

"Like a shot, I imagine. He likes your work."

"He cooks well."

"Yes, Mother. Military schools."

"Really? That explains it."

"Explains what?"

"He stands and moves like a soldier. Precise."

"I haven't noticed."

"Of course not, darling."

"Mother. . . ."

"I like your Chase, darling."

"He's not mine, Poppy."

"Better tell him that."

"I have. The man's deaf."

"The man has good taste."

"You're prejudiced."

"Slightly. Not that it matters."

"Gypsy, Corsair's sitting in the sink."

"Check his water dish, Mother."

"Chase, why do you keep letting Bucephalus inside?"

"Sorry, Rebecca, but he knocks."

"Do you let in every salesperson who knocks?"

"Only the ones with good legs."

"Chauvinist."

"Dyed-in-the-wool."

"Chase, what were you talking to Mother about? You look strange."

"I feel strange. She just told me the story of how Allen managed to catch her. No wonder you wouldn't tell me."

"Well, it's their story. Don't take it too much to heart, by the way."

"You mean, don't let it give me ideas?"

"Something like that."

"I wouldn't dare. You look like her, but you're not Rebecca. You'd come after me with a gun."

"I'm glad you realize that."

"Military schools don't produce idiots."

By the time Gypsy tumbled into bed that night, she was still laughing softly. The little party had broken up only an hour before, with Chase saying good night along with Rebecca and Allen.

Gypsy pushed Corsair off her foot and turned off the lamp, settling down to sleep.

The phone rang. Gypsy reached for it automatically. "Hello?"

"Did you dream about me last night?"

She smiled into the darkness. "I told you I would."

"Reality's better than dreams."

"Oh, really?"

"I could show you."

"I don't know who you are," she told him serenely.

"I could show you that too."

"It's better this way. Ships passing in the night, unseen."

"But lovers have to meet."

"It would destroy the mystery."

" 'But love is such a mystery,' " he quoted softly.

Gypsy found herself automatically quoting the last line of the verse. "And would you be 'such a constant lover'?"

"Eternally, love. Eternally. Sleep well."

Gypsy cradled the receiver slowly, gently. She plumped up her pillow and lay back, thinking whimsical thoughts. About a white horse and a masked rider. About an inept gardener and a marvelous cook. About a late-night caller who quoted obscure poetry and called her love.

About a lover.

FIVE

The old saying about time passing on winged feet had never meant anything to Gypsy until that next week. The days flew by.

Chase was in, out, and around. Going up the tree after Corsair became a morning ritual; no matter where Chase hid his keys (even under his pillow one night, he said), the cat always found them. Chase began to talk darkly about felines murdered in the night.

He didn't interfere unduly with Gypsy's work, although he insisted on making sure that she ate at regular intervals. So he either cooked, carted in a bag of "take-out" something, or took her out somewhere. He kept her laughing, continued his talk of seduction . . . and never once tried to follow through.

He kissed her occasionally, but Gypsy was never quite sure what kind of kiss it would

105

be or where it would land. A gentle kiss on her forehead, a playful kiss on her nose . . . or a hungry kiss that left her lips throbbing and her knees weak.

Always prone to talk to herself, Gypsy was fast approaching the point of answering herself as well.

And Chase was obviously having problems of his own. He stalked in late Tuesday afternoon, tightly reining the first sign of temper Gypsy had ever seen in him. With what looked like heroic patience he announced, "There's a white cat in my bedroom closet that has chosen to have three kittens in a box containing my new dinner jacket."

Looking up from the page she'd been proofing, Gypsy blinked at him in bewilderment. "Well, what do you want me to do about it?" she asked reasonably.

Chase hung on to control. "Corsair," he explained through gritted teeth, "is standing guard at the closet door, and won't let me near them."

Frowning, Gypsy said reproachfully, "You aren't supposed to disturb newborn kittens."

Chase looked toward the heavens imploringly. Gypsy went on in a puzzled voice. "Why wasn't your dinner jacket hanging up?

It should have been, you know."

"I didn't get the chance to hang it up. It was delivered yesterday; I just checked to make sure it was my order and left the open box in the bottom of the closet." He stared at her. "I thought you only had one cat."

"I do. She must be Corsair's girlfriend. I knew he had one around here, but I've never seen her."

"Couldn't we transfer the family over here?"

"With Bucephalus around? She'd only move them back, Chase. Cats are particular."

"Would you like me to tell you how much her nest is worth?" Chase asked politely.

Gypsy wasn't listening. "Chase, does she have blue eyes?"

He blinked. "I don't know. Corsair won't let me close enough to turn on the closet light, and it's dim in there. Why?"

"Well, if she's solid white and has blue eyes, she's probably deaf. I'll bet that's why Corsair's protecting her."

"Deaf?"

"It's fairly common. Some kind of genetic defect, I think."

He stared at her.

"There's cat food in the kitchen," Gypsy

murmured, trying not to laugh. "Help your-self."

"Gee, thanks." He left.

Chase apparently became accustomed to his new pets. He gave Gypsy periodic reports and complained of being unable to sleep at night because of squeaks and rustles in his closet. He also made a sort of peace with Corsair, since it was impossible to get to his closet through a hostile cat. But the morning key-ritual continued.

And Gypsy's "night lover" continued to call. More obscure poems were quoted, and the conversations became more and more suggestive. She looked forward to the tele-phone calls each night and found that she was sleeping better than ever before. The calls were . . . a nice way to end the day, Gypsy thought.

Whenever he thought she'd been working too hard, Chase pulled Gypsy away from her typewriter. For a meal. For a walk on the beach. She didn't protest because she wasn't far enough into her story to become obsessed by it. But she knew that, sooner or later, Chase would discover a witch with a capital B sitting at the desk where his laugh-ing companion had sat just the day before. She didn't look forward to that day.

In the meantime he kept coming up with

things for them to do together. On Thursday afternoon he announced his latest plan.

"It's a masquerade party. In Portland."

"Are you serious? I thought those things went out with hoop skirts."

"I'm serious. It's for charity. So be a good girl and rent a costume tomorrow."

"I'm without a car, remember."

"I'll loan you mine."

"Like to live dangerously, don't you?"

"Always."

Gypsy reflected. "A masquerade. What kind of costume should I get? Or does it matter?"

"It matters. Old West."

"It'd serve you right if I went dressed as Calamity Jane."

"Don't do that. Your gun and my sword would get all tangled up when we dance."

"Your what?"

"Sword."

"What Old West character wore a sword?"

"Wait and see."

"Beast. Just for that, I'll come as a saloon girl."

"With feathers?"

"And sequins."

"Oh, good."

"You'll have to fight the other cowboys off me with a stick," she warned him gravely.

"I'll use my sword. I've always wanted to challenge somebody to a duel."

"Murder?"

"An affair of honor," he corrected nobly.

"Only if he's bigger than you. Otherwise it's murder. And you're talking to someone who knows murder."

Chase perched on the corner of her desk, obviously willing to stay and talk for a while. "So tell me, what's the perfect murder weapon?"

"No such animal." She chewed on a knuckle thoughtfully, her chair leaning backward until it was in imminent danger of going over. "I've always wanted to use the jawbone of an ass as a murder weapon. Interesting, huh?"

"I think that's been done."

"Not recently."

"You'd know better than me."

"Naturally."

"What's your plot in this book?"

"I don't talk about them until they're finished."

"That's cruel. You know I'm a mystery buff."

"No exceptions."

"Orders from the muse?"

"I suppose."

"I'll rig a Chinese water torture."

"Go feed your cats."

"That's 'the unkindest cut of all.' "

Gypsy drove Chase's car — *very* carefully — into Portland on Friday to get a costume. She toyed with the idea of finding the briefest saloon-girl costume possible, but discarded the notion.

She wanted something else.

She found the something else in the first costume-rental shop listed in the Yellow Pages. So far, Chase had seen her in nothing but shorts or jeans, and she wanted to wear something feminine. And what could be more feminine than a long dress with a hoop skirt?

Gypsy didn't question her desire to look feminine. She wasn't questioning anything these days. And that was a bad sign. But she didn't want to question *that* either.

The boxes were loaded into the trunk of the Mercedes, and Gypsy left the rental shop. She ran a few errands in Portland, and then headed back toward the coast. It was late afternoon when she arrived back home.

She parked Chase's car in his driveway and collected the boxes from the trunk, absently putting the keys in the pocket of her jeans. Chase was nowhere to be seen;

she shrugged, then carried the boxes across to her house.

She hung the costume in her bedroom, put away the few odds and ends she'd bought, and then settled down in the living room with the book of poetry she'd found in a used bookstore. Obscure poems and poets. Her "night lover" had her on her mettle, and she wanted to refresh her memory. She ended up going through two more books from her shelves, discovering a treasure-trove in Donne and Shakespeare.

"What *are* you doing?"

"Reading poetry. You did say that the masquerade is tomorrow night, didn't you?" She looked up from her cross-legged position on the floor to peer at Chase over the tops of her study glasses.

"Tomorrow night it is." He slid his hands into the pockets of his jeans and leaned against the bookcase, gazing down at her with a smile that looked as if it were trying hard to hide. "Do your murderers read poetry to their victims at the eleventh hour?" he asked gravely.

Gypsy pushed the glasses back up her nose. "Are you kidding?" She narrowed her eyes expressively. "My murderers stalk their victims on cloven hooves."

"Mmm. Then why are you reading poetry?"

"I like poetry, peasant."

"I beg your pardon, I'm sure."

Gypsy pulled off the glasses and waved them magnanimously. "You're forgiven."

"Thank you. There's another pair on top of your head."

"What?"

"Another pair of glasses."

That explained his trying-not-to-smile expression, Gypsy thought. She pulled off the second pair and set them absently on the bottom shelf of the bookcase.

"Does it take two pairs for you to read poetry?" he asked politely.

"Never mind."

He went on conversationally. "I've counted eight pairs of glasses scattered throughout this house. All in strange places. Like the pair I found in the refrigerator yesterday."

"I wonder why I put them in there?" Gypsy murmured, more to herself than to him.

"I haven't the faintest idea, and I don't think I want to know."

"Smart man."

"But what I *would* like to know" — he pointed at the corner of her desk, where a

113

new acquisition was sitting — "is why you got *that* during your trip into Portland."

That was a statue of an eleven-inch-tall Buddha with a clock in its stomach. A broken clock.

Gypsy ran her fingers through her black curls and gave him a harassed look. "I asked myself that. *What do you want with a Buddha with a clock in his tummy?* No answer. I must have been possessed. There was a garage sale, and somehow or other . . . Anyway I paid five bucks for it." She shook her head darkly.

Chase reached down and pulled her to her feet. He removed the glasses from her hand and tossed them lightly onto the desk. Then he caught her in a tight bear hug. "Gypsy," he said whimsically, "I can't tell you what a delight you are to me."

She pulled back far enough to look up at him blankly. "Because I bought a Buddha?"

He laughed. "No, because you're you. I thought we'd cook out tonight; how do you like your steaks?"

"Cooked." Gypsy made no effort to disentangle herself from his embrace.

"There goes that sharp tongue again, Gypsy mine. You shouldn't sass your elders; you're liable to get paddled."

"Are you my elder? I didn't know."

"I'm thirty-two, brat."

"Methuselah."

He swatted her jean-clad bottom lightly. "How do you like your steak?"

"Well done. And stop hitting me!"

"It'll teach you not to sass me." Chase was unrepentant.

"I'll sic Bucephalus on you!" she threatened.

"I've been slipping him snacks for days now; that dog loves me like a brother."

Gypsy pushed against his chest, curiously pleased when she couldn't budge him. "Leave! People over thirty can't be trusted."

"That slogan went out of style years ago."

"Only because the people saying it reached thirty."

"Are you sassing me again?" he demanded.

"For all I'm worth."

He bent his head and kissed her suddenly. But it wasn't a gentle kiss. It was demanding, probing, possessive, and just short of violent. He kissed her as though he wanted — needed — to brand her as his for all time. The kiss lasted for brief seconds only, but Gypsy felt as though every nerve in her body had been lanced with sheer electricity.

Chase stared down at her. "Are you through sassing?" he asked hoarsely.

Gypsy nodded mutely, wondering dimly when she was going to start breathing again.

"Good." He lowered her gently to her former position on the floor. "You finish reading your poetry. I'll yell when I get the grill going."

She nodded again, and watched him turn away. When he'd gone, she gazed blindly down until a line of Donne's jumped out at her from the open book before her on the carpet. "Take me to you, imprison me. . . ."

Why did it suddenly make her ache inside?

He called again that night, and their conversation took a turning point. No longer seductively suggestive, it was filled with gentle whimsy.

It was somehow easier to open up to a husky voice on the telephone, easier to admit to and show vulnerability. Alone in her bedroom, lying in the darkness, she could be the sensitive woman who mourned the loss of heroes. . . .

"I've missed you," he breathed softly. "The sound of your voice haunts me, and yet I can't hear enough of it."

"You don't know me," she murmured in reply.

" 'Twice or thrice had I loved thee, before

I knew thy face or name,' " he quoted tenderly.

Gypsy smiled into the darkness. He'd read Donne as well. "You don't know me," she repeated.

"Then tell me what I should know."

"I don't . . ." Her voice trailed away.

"Do you love rainbows?" he asked gently. She smiled. "Yes."

"And the sound of rain in the morning?"

"Yes."

"Do you wish on stars?"

"I do now," she whispered, tears springing to her eyes.

"Then I know all that I should know," he said.

"Do you believe in unicorns?" she asked him.

"I do now," he replied.

"And life on other worlds?"

"Yes."

"And . . . heroes?"

"And heroes."

"I don't think you're real," she told him with a shaky laugh.

"I'm real, my love. Flesh and bone, heart and mind . . . and soul. And my soul aches for you."

Gypsy felt her heart stop for a moment and then pound on. What could she say to that? What could she possibly say?

But he didn't expect a response.

"Sleep well, my love. And dream of me."

She did.

It took Gypsy two hours to get into her costume late the next afternoon. She wasn't really accustomed to dresses of any kind, and even less to dresses fastened with tiny hooks and eyes, and beneath which were rather puzzling undergarments.

She had decided to stretch a point with the costume; otherwise, she'd have had to wear something like calico if she wanted to be authentic. And since she had a hunch about Chase's costume, she felt free to stretch a point. Besides — *Old West* covered a lot of territory.

Gypsy giggled over the shiftlike garment and the frilly bloomers, but the corset presented a problem. She had a small waist, but she'd been astonished at how much smaller it appeared after the assistant at the costume shop had laced her up in the corset. Being Gypsy, she'd had the corset included without a single thought as to who would lace her up at home.

She finally put it on backward, laced it up, and then spent a few comical moments holding her breath and tugging. With the

118

strings finally tied in a fierce knot, she collapsed on her bed, flushed and breathless.

No wonder the pictures of women in that era always looked so stiff, she thought. And no wonder genteel ladies were constantly swooning.

But once the dress was on, Gypsy understood why women had sacrificed comfort for the dictates of fashion.

The dress was black silk, and it rustled softly whenever she moved. Worn over a wide hoop — Gypsy had giggled for ten minutes after seeing herself in shift, bloomers, corset, and hoop — it was low-cut and off-the-shoulder. The corset nipped in her waist to a tiny span, and lifted her breasts until it seemed that a deep breath would get her arrested. She wasn't worried though; she could barely breathe anyway.

The dress was wicked for any era, and instantly branded her a scarlet woman in the era it pretended to belong to. The colorful splash of fake emeralds at her throat and dangling from her ears, however, loudly announced that she — or rather, her character — possessed wealth, and wealth could open doors even for scarlet women.

Gypsy had worked long and hard with her makeup, but was still faintly surprised to find that she had actually achieved a seductive look. The emeralds lent her gray eyes a green gleam, and the careful shading she'd done gave them a catlike slant. And the scrap of black silk that would serve as a mask only emphasized the seductive look.

"I look like a hussy," she told Corsair, who was sitting companionably at the foot of her bed, watching her. He'd stopped constantly guarding his family since Chase had proved to be reasonable.

"Is this what's called playing with fire, cat?" she asked him wryly.

Corsair yawned.

"Don't let me keep you awake," she begged politely.

By the time Chase knocked on the front door, Gypsy had donned the floor-length cloak and fastened it securely to hide the low neckline of her dress. Not that she was nervous about the cleavage, but there was no need to startle the man right off the bat, she decided mischievously.

Gypsy opened the door and gazed silently from the black-booted heels to the top of a Spanish-style hat. Her hunch had been right on target: He was dressed as Zorro.

"Are you going to run around tonight slashing Z's in the woodwork?" she asked him solemnly.

"Only if someone maligns your honor," he

replied with equal solemnity and a deep bow.

She started to warn him that just about anyone would malign her honor once they got a good look at her dress, but decided to await developments.

"Black suits you," he noted critically, head to one side as he studied her masked face. "As a matter of fact, you look beautiful. Why are your eyes green?"

Gypsy flicked a dangling earring with one finger. "It's the emeralds. And thank you."

"You're welcome. It's a long drive to Portland, so we'd better get started. Just as soon as you tell me where you left my car keys."

"Car keys. . . ."

It took Gypsy half an hour to locate the keys; she'd left them in the pocket of her jeans and had forgotten to return them to Chase. He waited patiently while she searched, but every time she passed him, he fingered the hilt of his sword and gave her a threatening look.

The sixty-some-odd-mile journey to Portland took less than an hour.

"Do you know what the speed limit is?"

"Of course, I know."

"No wonder you killed Daisy."

"Funny. Besides, it's this damn sword; it

keeps stabbing me in the foot."

"You're supposed to be wearing it on your *left* hip."

"Why?"

"You're right-handed."

"Oh. Remind me to change it around when we get there."

"Right. Are you sure you'll be able to dance in that thing?"

"Of course I will." There was a pause. "The couples dancing near us'll have to watch their step though."

The masquerade was being held in a huge recreation center on the outskirts of Portland. The charity involved was one for needy children. From the looks of the size of the crowd that had turned out, whatever goal had been set for this fund-raising event, it had been reached easily. Costumes were varied and ranged from the sublime to the ridiculous. Royalty from the Court of St. James vied with those of other European countries, and clashed with various fuzzy creatures from recent movies and assorted fairy-tale and nursery-rhyme characters. There was even one giant of a man who was dressed as Paul Bunyan, and kept wandering around asking if anybody'd seen his ox.

Refreshments had been set out along one wall, and the buzz and laughter of a hundred conversations filled the tremendous room. A small band of musicians tuned their instruments screechily in one corner.

Gypsy winced at a particularly discordant clash as Chase, standing behind her, removed her cloak and handed it over to the cloakroom attendant. "Are we supposed to be able to dance to that?" she asked wryly, turning to face him.

Chase's mouth fell open.

Suddenly remembering her dress, Gypsy fought to hide her smile. "Didn't know I was so well blessed, did you?" she asked him gravely.

His eyes lifted to her face, and he laughed. "Gypsy, you say the damnedest things!"

"What's a little bluntness between friends?"

"Oh, I wholeheartedly approve. Of the bluntness — and the dress. Shall we check out the refreshments?"

"Yes. I'm dying of thirst, but I won't be able to eat anything."

"Why not?" He took her arm and began leading her toward the refreshments.

"I'll tell you about it someday." Her voice was rueful.

He looked at her curiously. "Now you've got me wondering."

Gypsy thought of her afternoon's struggle,

and her lips twitched. "Never mind."

"Gypsy . . ."

"Hang onto your sword, will you? You just stabbed that Louis in the shin."

"I wondered why he was glaring at me." Chase handed her a cup of punch with his free hand. "And don't try to weasel out of it; why can't you eat something?"

Gypsy glanced furtively around to make sure no one was close enough to overhear. "It's my corset," she told him in a stage whisper.

"Your what?"

"My corset. I can barely breathe, much less eat." Gypsy thoroughly enjoyed the struggle going on on his face.

After a moment he set his own cup of punch on the table, released his death grip on the hilt of his sword, and solemnly measured the span of her waist with both hands. "Yep. It's definitely smaller."

"Looks great to me," announced a strange masculine voice over Chase's left shoulder.

Chase turned suddenly, stabbing another Louis (or was it the same one?) in the shin as he greeted the tall man who'd come up behind him. "Jake, the last I heard, you were building something in Texas."

"Surprise! I finished building it."

Introduced to Jake Thomas a moment

later, Gypsy's first impression was that Chase's builder friend was an absolute nut. He was big and rawboned, his size and obviously cheerful personality perfectly suited to his lumberjack costume. It took Gypsy only a moment to realize that he was the Paul Bunyan in search of his ox.

"You're the one who writes those mysteries Chase is always raving about, aren't you?" Jake asked Gypsy after the introduction.

Gypsy looked up at Chase in surprise, only to find him gazing studiously into space. "Well, I write mysteries," she answered Jake.

"You don't look it," Jake told her gravely, and at her expressive grimace, added, "You've heard that before, I take it?"

"Innumerable times."

A black cat wandered up just then, holding on to her long tail to avoid having it stepped on. She was about Gypsy's size, with a petite figure and blond hair escaping from beneath her ear cap. And she had large blue eyes that looked dumb but were obviously lying.

"Jake, how dare you leave me in the clutches of that King George? He kept bumping me with his stomach and stepping on my tail."

Laughing, Jake introduced Gypsy to his fiancée, Sarah Foxx. Chase she obviously knew, since she stood on tiptoe to kiss his cheek lightly.

"You write mysteries?" Sarah asked in surprise, studying Gypsy. "You —"

"— don't look like it," the other three chorused.

"I seem to be redundant," Sarah observed wryly.

"That's all right," Gypsy told her. "I'm getting used to it."

"I'll bet." Sarah gave her a friendly grin. "That's the price you and I pay for looking as if we can't string two words together."

Gypsy looked interested. "What do you do?"

"I'm a psychologist."

Gypsy felt an immediate affinity for the other woman. "Isn't it terrible? That nature played this awful trick and made us look dumb, I mean?"

"Yes, but it has its advantages. People are always bending over backward to do things for us because we look so helpless."

"There is that," Gypsy agreed thoughtfully.

Chase sighed in manful long-suffering. "Don't you two start talking about the failings of mankind, or Jake and I won't get to dance."

Sarah looked solemnly at him and said, totally deadpan, "You and Jake can dance if you like. It might look a little odd, but if *you* don't mind . . ."

"Cute, that's cute." Chase took a giggling Gypsy firmly by the arm. "Dance with me, Gypsy mine, before Sarah puts us both on her couch."

The musicians had struck up a waltz, and he swept her regally out onto the floor. One *ouch!* and two muffled *dammit*'s followed them.

"Chase, you're going to have to take off that sword."

"Zorro without his sword? Don't be ridiculous."

"They'll throw us out."

"They can't afford to refund our money."

"You're making enemies."

"We're supposed to be dancing in romantic silence here."

"How can we dance in romantic silence with curses following us all around the floor? See? You just stuck Louis again."

"He'll learn to keep out of my way."

"Chase —"

"All right, shrew! I'll take it off and let the cloakroom attendant keep an eye on it. But you're coming with me. I don't want anyone stealing you away from me."

"Who'd want to do that?"

"Louis. Revenge."

"Thanks a lot."

"You're welcome."

Six

Louis obviously wasn't in the market for revenge that night. As a matter of fact, he kept a respectful distance from Gypsy and Chase — sword or no sword. A couple of braver souls attempted to cut in on Chase, but retreated in some confusion when Zorro sneered at them.

Between dances Gypsy and Chase stood talking to Jake and Sarah. The two couples were apparently on the same wavelength; there was none of the normal awkwardness or guardedness of new acquaintances. By evening's end Gypsy knew that she had two new friends.

She was also a bit unnerved to realize that her response to Chase during the evening had been very much like Sarah's to Jake; teasing, playful, bantering. It shouldn't have surprised her, since the same type of thing had gone on since the day she'd met him. But it did surprise her.

It surprised her because she had never looked at their relationship objectively — from the outside, so to speak. But in comparing them to the other couple, the similarities were startling. It was as though she and Chase were lovers of long standing. Companionable, playful, teasing, they reacted to each other with the certain knowledge of two people who were very close.

It gave Gypsy food for thought.

The party broke up around midnight, with invitations extended and accepted for a barbecue at Chase's house on Sunday afternoon, and the two couples went their separate ways: Sarah and Jake to the apartment they shared in Portland, and Gypsy and Chase toward the coast.

It was silent in the car for most of the trip, a companionable silence that neither chose to break. Gypsy was occupied by various thoughts and by the rumbling in her stomach; she had eaten nothing since breakfast, and was by now heartily cursing the binding, uncomfortable corset. She was also beginning to wonder how on earth she was going to get out of the thing; she'd never been very good with knots. And along the same lines was her dress; the tiny hooks and eyes had been nearly impossible to fasten, and she wasn't at all sure that she could *un*fasten them without tearing the rented costume.

A solution occurred to her, and Gypsy considered it idly. Dangerous. Definitely dangerous. Playing with fire for sure. She wondered why she wasn't at all concerned any longer about burning her fingers. It might have had something to do with the kiss Chase had bestowed during the un-masking at the party. It had been a definitely fiery kiss — a first cousin to Vesuvius. Her lips were still tingling.

And after that . . . why worry about burning her fingers?

Chase parked the Mercedes in his drive-way, and they walked across to Gypsy's door. She located her key in the string purse dangling from her wrist, and Chase un-locked the door.

"Is the evening over, or are you going to ask me in?" he inquired politely.

"The evening is young. Besides, I have a favor to ask. Come in, please."

"A favor?" Chase followed her into the dimly lighted den, his cloak and mask land-ing beside Gypsy's on one of the chairs. "Your wish is, of course, my command."

"I'm so glad. It's a . . . delicate favor."

"So much the better." Just as she turned to face him he caught her in his arms. A

131

faint, lazy smile lifted the corners of his mouth. "Gentlemanly courtesy aside, though, I'm afraid I have other things on my mind right now."

"Chase —"

He kissed her, and Gypsy promptly forgot all about the favor. She might have been vague, but she wasn't stupid; what woman would pass up an opportunity to revisit Vesuvius? She felt his hands lifting, the fingers threading through her black curls, and her own arms lifted to slide round his waist. His lips toyed with hers for a brief moment; gentle, sensitive. And then he abruptly accepted the unconscious invitation of her parting lips, deepening the kiss in a sudden surge of curiously yearning hunger.

Gypsy abandoned herself to sensation. A part of her stood back and watched, both disturbed and fascinated by the woman who gave herself up totally to addictive sensations. She felt one of his hands move to caress the side of her neck lightly, his thumb rhythmically brushing her jawline; his free hand slid slowly down her back, over bare flesh that tingled at the touch. The warmth of his mouth seduced, impelled, made her forget everything except the need to have more of this. . . .

The phone rang.

Gypsy wanted to ignore it. She *tried* to ignore it. But it was ringing persistently, and finally Chase raised his head with a groan.

"Oh, Lord! And we were doing so well too!"

She stared up at him, dazed, for a long moment, then firmly got a grip on herself. A warlock. He was definitely a warlock. She moved toward the phone as he reluctantly released her. Clearing her throat as she lifted the receiver, Gypsy managed a weak "Hello?"

"You've been out!" a wounded male voice accused sadly.

Gypsy slammed the phone down so hard and fast that she nearly caught her fingers beneath it. "Oh, God . . ." she whispered to herself, appalled. A stranger? Some nut had been calling her, and she'd —

"Who was that?" Chase had come up behind her and began to nuzzle the side of her neck.

"Uh . . . wrong number." She was glad he couldn't see her face; it probably scaled the limits of human shock.

He chuckled softly. "You obviously have no patience with wrong numbers; somebody's ears are still ringing."

Apparently not; the phone began ringing again.

Gypsy didn't move, she just stared at it silently.

"Persistent devil." Chase made a move toward the phone. "Want me to . . . ?"

"No!" Hastily Gypsy picked up the receiver, trying to ignore Chase's startled look. "Hello?"

"Darling, why did you —"

"I can't talk now," she interrupted hurriedly, and hung up before another word could be uttered. There was a dead silence from behind her. She decided not to turn around.

"Should I ask?" he inquired finally in a mild voice.

"No." Gypsy sought hastily for something to divert his mind. Although why she should feel so guilty . . . ! And who the *hell* had been calling her all this time? she wondered. "Uh . . . Chase, about that favor . . . ?"

"I'd forgotten. Other things on my mind, I'm afraid." His voice was disconcertingly formal. "What is it?"

Gypsy mentally flipped a coin. She lost. Or won. Or maybe, she thought miserably, it didn't matter either way. She arranged her face and turned to gaze up at him. "Would you please help me get these clothes

134

off?" she requested baldly.

It diverted his mind.

Chase blinked at least three times, and Gypsy could definitely see some sort of struggle going on beneath his tightly held expression. And then he relaxed, and she knew that she had won after all. A jade twinkle was born in his eyes.

"I thought we were doing well," he murmured.

Gypsy fixed him with a plaintive look. "I don't think I can get them off by myself. The dress has tiny hooks and eyes, and the corset . . . well, I tied the strings in a knot. And I'm not very good with knots," she added seriously.

He sat down on the arm of the couch and folded his arms across his chest, bowing his head and laughing silently.

"It's very uncomfortable!" she told him severely.

"Sorry." He wiped his eyes with one hand. "It's just . . . dammit, Gypsy — Cyrano de Bergerac couldn't romance you with a straight face!"

"Oh, really?" She lifted a haughty brow at him.

"Really." He pulled her into his lap, and both of them watched, totally deadpan, as her hoop skirt shot into the air and poised there like a quivering curtain.

She turned her head to stare at him. "You may have a point."

"Yes."

"This never happens to heroines in the movies."

"Uh-huh." Chase looked as though his expressionless face was the result of enormous effort and clenched teeth.

"They *never* get stuck in their dresses," Gypsy persisted solemnly.

"God forbid."

"Or lose control of their hoops."

He choked.

"Or have to put their corsets on backward."

Chase bit his bottom lip with all the determination of a straight man.

"Or ask a man, with absolutely no delicacy, to take their clothes off." Gypsy reflected a moment, then amended gravely, "Except a certain kind of heroine, of course."

"Of course," Chase agreed unsteadily.

There was a moment of silence, broken only by a peculiar sound. Gypsy looked down at her tightly corseted stomach disgustedly. "Or have stomachs that growl like volcanos," she finished mournfully.

It was too much for Chase. He collapsed

backward on the couch, pulling Gypsy with him, unheeding and uncaring that her hoop was doing a fan dance in the air above them. He was laughing too hard to notice. So was Gypsy.

She finally struggled up, fighting her hoop every step of the way and sending Chase into fresh paroxysms of mirth. Sitting on the edge of the couch and clutching the hoop to keep it grounded, she requested breathlessly, "Please unfasten this damn dress — it hurts to laugh!"

Gaining a finger-and-toe-hold on his amusement, Chase rose on an elbow and began working with the tiny fastenings of her dress. They were undone much faster than they'd been done, and she was soon rising to her feet and wrestling yards of material up over her head. When she emerged, flushed and panting, she tossed the dress carelessly onto a chair and looked at Chase.

No man had ever beheld a woman stripping with more appreciation, she decided wryly. Chase was all but rolling on the couch, and if a man could die laughing, he was clearly about to.

She posed prettily, one hand holding the bare hoop and the other patting tousled curls in vain. The vision of herself in shift, bloomers, corset, and hoop obviously affected Chase just as it had her.

"I thought all men liked to see women in their underwear," she said provocatively.

Chase gathered breath for one sentence. "Take it off," he gasped. "Take it *all* off!"

Gypsy placed hands at hips and affected a Mae West drawl. "You think I do this for free, buster? There's a cover charge, you know."

He laughed harder.

Uncaring of the ludicrous embellishments of fake emeralds dangling from her ears and around her neck, and delicate black high-heeled slippers, Gypsy discarded — with some difficulty — the hoop and went over to sit on the couch beside Chase. He'd struggled to a sitting position and was once more wiping his eyes.

"Pity you left your sword in the car," she said, struggling with the stubborn knot on her corset.

"Sorry," he murmured unsteadily. "I didn't know you'd need it."

Gypsy sighed, kicked off her slippers, and sat back, giving Chase a pleading look. "D'you mind? If I don't take a deep breath in the next few seconds, I'm going to be the first woman of the twentieth century to suffocate because of a corset."

Not bothering to hide his grin, Chase reached for the stubborn knot. "In the twentieth century?" he queried gravely.

"You can't make me believe that nobody ever died in one of these things. The lengths women go to for fashion!"

"You should try wearing a sword," he said.

"No, thanks. Besides, swords were for self-defense, not fashion. How could a woman defend herself with a corset?"

"It obviously gave her an edge in defending her honor," he pointed out, tugging at the stubborn knot. "I don't understand how the population of the world managed to increase during this stage of fashion."

"Carefully," she murmured. "Ouch!"

"Sorry. Maybe we'll need the sword after all. Could you inhale a little?"

Gypsy gave him a look reserved for those persons one step below the moron level in intelligence. "Are you kidding?"

"Cyrano would definitely find it an uphill struggle," Chase murmured wryly. "What are those things called?" He gestured.

"Bloomers."

There was a moment of silence, then Chase said carefully, "I see."

Gypsy crossed her ankles and linked her fingers together behind her neck, affecting a pose of comfort. "If my father were to walk in right now . . ."

"Yes?" Chase asked politely.

"Well, think about the picture we're presenting. Here I am in a very undressed state, with a man dressed all in black and bending over me in a very suggestive and villainous pose. . . ."

"Do you want to sleep in your corset?"

"I was just making conversation. It's not easy to sit here calmly and watch you trying to take my clothes off, you know."

"And you not even struggling! What's the world coming to?" he said in a shocked voice.

"Terrible, isn't it?"

"Definitely." He sighed. "I'm going to have to cut the strings."

"Oh, no, you don't! This thing's rented."

"What could a couple of strings cost?" he asked reasonably.

"It's the principle of the thing. Could you just try a little while longer? Please?"

"You like watching me suffer," he accused wryly.

"Are you suffering?" she asked interestedly.

"I'm dying by inches. I've been struggling to keep my hands to myself all night, and now here I am. You're at my mercy, dressed in a corset, bloomers, and some kind of top that I can see right through —"

"Keep your eyes on the corset," Gypsy muttered, embarrassed for the first time.

The jade eyes gleamed with mischief — and something else. "You're blushing," he announced, chuckling.

"I am not. If my face is red, it's due to lack of oxygen. I'm telling you — this thing's killing me!"

"Then you'll have to let me cut — There! That's got it. Now you can breathe again."

Gypsy took a deep, ecstatic breath while he removed the corset and tossed it on top of the dress and hoop. "Air!" she murmured blissfully. "Both lungs full. If you ever take me to another masquerade," she added flatly, "I'll go as a writer."

"I'll remember that." Chase's mind didn't seem to be on what he was saying. His left hand was resting on her flat stomach, separated from her skin only by the almost transparent linen of her shift. His jade eyes, darkening almost to black were gazing into hers.

Suddenly wordless, Gypsy watched as he leaned toward her slowly. She wondered dimly at the abrupt cessation of laughter, of humor. And marveled at how quickly her heart had leaped to a reckless rhythm. And then all academic wonderings ceased, faded into nothingness.

His lips touched hers lightly, and Gypsy was just about to abandon reason willingly when she felt him shaking with silent laughter. He lifted his head, then dropped it again abruptly, resting his forehead against her stomach.

"Poor Cyrano," he murmured helplessly. "Oh, poor Cyrano!"

Gypsy was bewildered for a moment, but then she both felt and heard her empty stomach rumbling. So much for the fires of ardor! she thought. "Sorry," Gypsy said with a sigh. "I haven't eaten since breakfast."

"So I gathered." He rose to his feet, still chuckling, and offered her a hand. "Come on, Pauline."

"As in *The Perils of?*" she inquired dryly, accepting the helping hand.

"Well, you've got to admit that you're batting a thousand," he pointed out ruefully. "I don't know what you've got in the fridge, but —"

"Tons of stuff," she interrupted, leading the way to the kitchen without a thought of her decidedly strange hostess outfit. "I called a takeout place this afternoon with a huge order; I had a feeling I'd be starving by the time we got back. Chinese food."

"At two a.m.?" Chase protested weakly.

"When do *you* eat Chinese food?" she asked politely, busily removing various boxes and cartons from the refrigerator.

He sighed. "Another stupid question."

"Can you get that pitcher of tea?"

"Tea on Sat— No, it's Sunday, isn't it? And here I thought you were breaking with tradition willingly."

"Have an egg roll."

"Might as well." He sighed again. "My plans for the evening seem to be all shot to hell."

"Sorry."

"You sound it. Pass the soy sauce, please."

Half an hour later, Chase finally spoke again, diverting Gypsy's thoughts from her stomach and lungs — both full and content for the first time in hours.

"Gypsy?"

"Mmmm?" She bit into her third egg roll with relish.

"Could you at least button the top button?"

Startled, she instinctively looked down to see that her shift was displaying more of her charms than her dress had. Before she could say anything, he was going on conversationally.

"It's not that I hate looking, you understand. But since the end result of this

Chinese culinary retribution is bound to be acute indigestion, I don't think I really need to add skyrocketing blood pressure to my sleepless night."

Gypsy hastily buttoned the top button. "Sorry."

"Think nothing of it," he begged politely. Five minutes later he rose abruptly and left the kitchen without a word. When he returned, he was carrying her black cloak, which he dropped around her shoulders. "Not enough coverage," he said gruffly.

She fastened the cloak, hoping that he didn't think she'd been deliberately teasing him. "Chase, I'm sorry. I didn't mean —"

"I know," he said with a sigh, resuming his seat. "If I've learned anything about you, Gypsy mine, it's that the obvious answer is never the correct one."

"Is that good or bad?"

"I'll answer that question when *I* find out the answer."

Gypsy followed him to the front door some time later, feeling curiously vulnerable and not sure why. She held on to the cloak and gazed up at him as he opened the door, wondering if he was disappointed at the unplanned turn the evening had taken. She couldn't tell from his expression.

"Remember the barbecue tomorrow — I

mean, today. Jake and Sarah will be at my place around three."

She nodded. "I'll remember."

"It's been . . . an unusual evening, Gypsy mine." He grinned suddenly. "I don't think I ever enjoyed an evening half as much in my life. Has anyone ever told you that you're something different?"

"No." The relief in her voice was obvious even to her.

"An oversight, I'm sure." He bent his head to kiss her quickly, adding in a whisper, "And you look cute as hell in bloomers." With a cheerful wave he vanished into the night.

Gypsy slowly closed and locked the door, smiling to herself. She went through the house to the kitchen. She cleaned up in her usual manner, dropping cartons into the trash can and anything not made of paper into the sink. She let Bucephalus and Corsair in from the backyard, fed them (ignoring Corsair's irritated grumbles at being left outside for so long), and went up to bed.

"You hung up on me," he told her sadly.

Gypsy rubbed sleep-blurred eyes and stared at her bedside clock. She'd been in bed half an hour. "Who *are* you?" she

145

demanded, by now more angry and frustrated than horrified.

"I'm yours, my love —"

"Stop it!" she snapped.

"You're angry with me?"

"What do you think?" she asked witheringly. "Some *nut* calls me every night, and I'm supposed to be entranced?"

"Last night you —"

"Last night," she interrupted, "I thought I knew who you were."

"But you know who I am," he murmured whimsically. "We meet every night in your dreams."

"Quit it!"

"You belong to me."

"I'm calling the police."

"Mine."

She hung up. Hard.

The phone rang. And rang. Gypsy finally picked it up with a rueful sense of great-oaks-from-little-acorns-grow. Why had she ever started this?

" 'The day breaks not, it is my heart,' " he whispered.

"Stop quoting Donne, dammit," she ordered.

"So cruel. . . ."

Gypsy could feel herself weakening. Whoever he was, this man had seen the vulnerable side of her. And she wondered dimly why she was so sure that he had shown her a side of himself that no one else had ever seen. It had to be Chase. But how *could* it be? Nothing made sense!

"Stop calling me," she heard herself pleading.

"Would you ask me to stop breathing? It's the same, my love. The very same. I'd die. I love you."

"Don't love me. I . . . I'm in love with someone else." She cradled the receiver gently.

In the darkness of her bedroom Gypsy slid from the bed and dressed in jeans and a sweat shirt. She barely heard the phone begin to ring again as she left the room.

With Bucephalus as escort she went through the house to the kitchen, and then out into the yard. She crossed to the stairway down to the beach. Moments later she was sitting in her favorite seat and gazing out over a moonlit ocean, the big dog at her feet. She listened to the muted roar of the surf; she looked up to count the stars, wishing on a few; she might even have cried a little bit.

She thought about loving Chase.

Gypsy wasn't quite herself at the barbecue

later that day. She might have been developing a cold after sitting on a windy beach for the better part of a cool June night. Or it might have been lack of sleep. Or it might have been a last defensive gesture in a battle lost for good.

Whatever it was, Chase and her two new friends obviously noticed.

Being Gypsy, she couldn't pretend that everything was fine. She couldn't hide her almost nervous silences in response to Chase's teasing. She couldn't recapture the light bantering of the past days. And she couldn't help but stiffen at his lightest touch.

As the barbecue progressed his jade eyes began to follow her with an anxious, puzzled expression, and he asked her more than once what was wrong. She always answered with a meaningless smile and a swift change of subject.

By the time Gypsy picked her way through the meal of excellent barbecued ribs, baked potatoes, rolls, and crispy salad, Sarah had obviously seen enough. Laughing, she ordered the men (who had cooked) to do the cleaning up, seized Gypsy's arm in a companionable grip, and led her across the yard to the railing at the cliff.

"If you'll forgive an old, outworn cliché,"

she told the other woman ruefully, "the atmosphere between you and Chase is thick enough to cut with a blunt knife. You two have a fight? Or am I being incurably nosy?"

Having seen more than enough of the ocean the night before, Gypsy turned her back on the view and leaned against the railing. She smiled slightly and murmured, "No to both questions."

Sarah was silent for a moment. "Forgive me if I'm probing — a psychologist's stock-in-trade, I'm afraid — but can I help?"

"Is your couch free?" Gypsy managed lightly.

"For a friend in need? Always." Sarah leaned back against the railing and pulled a pack of cigarettes and a lighter from the pocket of the man's shirt she was wearing over a halter top. "Dreadful habit. Want one?"

"Thanks." Gypsy accepted a light.

"I didn't think you smoked," Sarah said.

"I quit three years ago."

"Uh-huh. But now . . . ?"

"Am I on your couch?" When Sarah nodded with a smile, Gypsy murmured, "I need a temporary crutch, I suppose." She blew a smoke ring and concentrated on it.

"Why?"

"To keep from falling flat on my face.

Although I think it's too late to prevent that."

"Falling as in 'in love'?"

"Are you that perceptive or am I that obvious?" Gypsy asked wryly.

"A little of both. You watch him when he isn't watching you. And another woman always knows." She paused. "You're scared." It was a statement.

"Terrified," Gypsy admitted almost inaudibly.

"Why? Chase is a wonderful man." She smiled when Gypsy looked at her. "I've known him longer than I've known Jake; he introduced us."

Gypsy wondered suddenly — an inescapable feminine wondering — and Sarah obviously understood; her smile widened.

"No, there was nothing serious between Chase and me. Just friendship. He's been searching ever since I've known him. Last night I realized that he wasn't searching any longer."

Gypsy fixed all her concentration on grinding the stub of her cigarette beneath one sandal.

Sarah went on slowly, thoughtfully. "He's been lonely, I think. His upbringing . . . well, he missed a lot. Don't get me wrong — Chase and his father have a very good

150

relationship. But he missed being part of a family. He missed the carefree, irresponsible years. I don't think he's ever done a reckless thing in his life."

Gypsy, thinking of a masked rider on the beach, smiled in spite of herself.

Sarah was obviously observing her closely. "Or maybe I'm wrong about that. You've been good for him, Gypsy."

Gypsy moved involuntarily, not quite sure that she wanted to hear this; not quite sure she could stand to hear it.

"You've unlocked a part of his personality." Sarah's voice was quiet and certain. "He was so relaxed last night, so cheerful and humorous. I've never seen him like that before. And he looked at you as if you were the pot of gold at the end of the rainbow."

"Please . . ." Gypsy murmured.

"What is it? What's the problem?"

"Me," Gypsy said starkly. "I'm the problem. I'm afraid — very much afraid — that I'll ruin things between us."

"How?"

"My writing." Gypsy showed Sarah a twisted smile. "He doesn't understand — and I don't think you will." She fumbled for an explanation. "Sometimes I get . . . obsessed. The story fills my mind until there's no room for anything else. For days or weeks at a time." She laughed shortly. "A friend with a couple of psychology courses under his belt told me once that I had a split personality."

"No," Sarah disagreed dryly. "Just an extremely creative mind. One out of every ten writers goes through roughly the same thing." She smiled when Gypsy gave her a look of surprise. "Creative minds fascinate scientists and shrinks; research has been done, believe me. You're not alone."

It was strangely reassuring, Gypsy thought. "But can Chase adapt to those kinds of mood swings? Sarah, I'm an absolute shrew! My own parents couldn't live with me once I started writing. And I'm no bargain when I'm *not* obsessed! I can't cook, I hate housework, I'm untidy to a fault — totally disorganized."

"Has any of this bothered Chase so far?" Sarah asked reasonably.

"No. But we're not living together."

"I'll bet he's around a lot though."

"Yes, but it's not the same."

"True." Sarah lifted a quizzical brow. "You won't thank me for pointing out that you're crossing your bridges before you come to them."

Gypsy sighed. "Meaning that all these rocks I'm throwing in my path may turn out to be more imagined than real, and why don't I give it a chance?"

"Something like that."

"Let's drag out another cliché. I'm afraid of getting hurt."

"Welcome to the human race." Sarah's voice was as sober as Gypsy's had been.

"Close my eyes and jump, huh?"

"Either that — or don't take the chance. And spend the rest of your life wondering if it would have been worth it." After a moment of silence Sarah added softly, "Some smart fellow once said something about it being better to have loved and lost. . . . I have a sneaking suspicion that he knew what he was talking about. But I don't think you'll lose."

"Why not?"

"Because I think you'll find that Chase is as adaptable as a stray cat. I think you'll find that he'll treasure the laughter *and* the fights, that he may even make it easier for you. I know he'll try."

"And I couldn't ask for more than that," Gypsy said softly.

The two women smiled at each other, and Gypsy added wryly, "Keep a couple of hours of couch time open, will you, friend? I just may need them."

Sarah laughed. "I'll do that. But I don't

think you'll need them. Shall we join the menfolk, friend? Jake should be swearing a blue streak by now; he hates cleaning up as much as you do."

"*Nobody* hates it as much as I do."

"Better hang on to Chase, then. With him it's sheer habit."

"Military schools have their uses."

And on that light note they joined the men.

SEVEN

Gypsy relaxed a bit during the next few hours. She was still thoughtful, introspective, but able to respond naturally to Chase. And she no longer stiffened when he touched her. Chase was patently relieved, although obviously still puzzled.

A late afternoon shower sent them inside around five, where they sprawled in various positions in the den and commenced a spirited game of charades. Sarah was the hands-down winner with her comical silent rendition of "My Old Kentucky Home" and received a standing ovation from the others. A fire was kindled in the fireplace as the rain continued outside, and Sarah and Jake went happily to raid Chase's kitchen for popcorn.

Gypsy sat silently on the couch, trying not to think too much about the jade eyes gazing up at her. Chase was lying on the couch with his head in her lap, and she could feel the steady beat of his heart beneath the hand resting on his chest. She stared into the fire.

"All day long," Chase said in a musing voice, "I've had this weird feeling, Gypsy mine."

Reluctant to meet his eyes, Gypsy nonetheless looked down. "About what?" she asked lightly.

"It's hard to explain." Chase toyed absently with her fingers. "As if . . . Juliet was about to shove Romeo off the balcony. As if Cleopatra told Marc Antony to walk the plank of her barge. As if Lois Lane asked Superman to take a flying leap."

Gypsy couldn't help but smile.

"As if you were trying to find some way of saying good-bye to me, Gypsy mine," he finished quietly.

She felt the utter stillness of the room, the level, searching gaze of his eyes, and her smile died. She shook her head slowly. "No."

He lifted her hand to cradle it against his cheek. "I'm glad." His voice was husky. A faint twinkle lighted the darkness of his eyes. "Besides — I wouldn't let you run me off with a loaded gun. Don't you know that by now?"

"Masterful," she murmured in response, her free hand unconsciously stroking his thick copper hair.

"Always." He pressed his lips briefly to the palm of her hand. "Which reminds me, about that phone call last night . . ."

Gypsy's faint smile remained. This was one subject she had been prepared for. "What about it?"

"That's just it: what about it? Why do I get the feeling I have a rival for your affections?"

"Sheer imagination."

"Will you tell me who it was?" He wouldn't be put off.

"Can't. I don't know myself." Her smile widened at his skeptical look. "I swear. It was my — uh — mystery lover. He calls every night." She carefully studied Chase's blank look; if he was acting, he deserved an Oscar, she thought wryly.

"Have you called the police?" he demanded.

"No." Gypsy wasn't about to explain *that.*

"Gypsy —"

"He's harmless, Chase. Besides . . . I like him."

Chase stared at her. "Maybe *I* should start calling you," he muttered.

"Maybe you should. And muffle your voice a bit."

"What? Why?" He looked thoroughly bewildered.

"Never mind." Gypsy looked up as Sarah and Jake entered with the popcorn. "Oh, good. Popcorn!"

Both the rain and the other couple had gone by eleven that night, after a late supper of leftover barbecue and a shoot-'em-up western on television. After Sarah and Jake had driven off, Gypsy felt more than a little let down when Chase solemnly offered to walk her home. She wondered irritably if he was trying to drive her crazy, then thought of the night before with a smothered giggle. Well, maybe he had cause!

As soon as they stepped out onto the porch, Chase stopped her with a frown. "You'll get your feet wet." As though she were contemplating a walk across crushed glass, he added, "Sandals are no protection." He swung her easily into his arms and started across the darkened lawn.

Gypsy linked her fingers together at the nape of his neck. "Let me guess." Her voice was grave. "Sir Walter Raleigh? The White Knight?"

"The former."

"No cape to lay across a puddle?" she asked in a wounded voice.

"No puddle," he pointed out. "And the

158

cape's rented."

"Details, details," she said airily.

"Don't pick on me when I'm trying to be heroic," he complained mildly.

"Sorry. Shall I change the subject, Walter?" She felt his arms tighten, and added hastily, "I'll change the subject. I've been meaning to ask you what you named your cat."

"She's not my cat, she's Corsair's cat. And he can have her back whenever he wants her."

"Uh-huh. The mailman told me Friday that you'd been asking around to see if she has a home hereabouts. And you ran an ad in the paper too."

"Busybody," Chase muttered.

Gypsy ignored the interruption. "So you found out that she's homeless?"

He sighed. "Not anymore."

"I thought so. What did you name her?"

If a man could squirm while walking and carrying a grown although pint-size woman, Chase squirmed. "Cat."

"Try again," she requested solemnly.

He sighed again. "Angel. Dammit."

Gypsy bit back a giggle. "Those blue eyes get 'em every time," she said soulfully.

Not really uncomfortable, Chase laughed softly. "Corsair's obviously been talking to

159

her; she thinks she's a queen. I've moved the family into one of the spare bedrooms, and she keeps trying to move them back. One of us is going to give up sooner or later."

"Bet I know which one."

Chase dipped her threateningly over a very wet hedge. "And just which one do you bet it'll be?" he asked politely.

"Angel, of course." Gypsy giggled. "I have every faith in your perseverance, Walter."

"Smart lady." He stepped onto her front porch and set her gently on her feet. But he didn't release her. "Busy tomorrow?"

Gypsy managed to nod firmly, even though she couldn't seem to make her fingers remove themselves from his neck. "I have to work. I've fallen behind."

"My fault?" he asked wryly.

"No. The first half of a book is always slow." She hesitated, wanting to warn him of what would surely come, but dimly aware that it was something he'd have to find out for himself.

"You'd better get some sleep, then." One finger lightly touched the faint purple shadows beneath her eyes. "You look tired."

"I'm not." Gypsy felt heat sweep up her throat at the hasty reply. But the truth was that she *didn't* feel tired. She felt on edge, restless, and sleep was the last thing on her mind.

Unfortunately Chase apparently wasn't picking up undercurrents tonight.

"Good night, Gypsy mine."

He kissed her. On the nose.

Leaning back against the closed front door after he'd gone, she automatically turned the deadbolt and fastened the night latch.

Dammit.

She frowned as Bucephalus came into the hallway and wagged a long tail at her. "Out?" she queried dryly. Bucephalus woofed softly.

Sighing, Gypsy went through the house to the kitchen, letting him out and Corsair in. "You're wet, cat," she muttered. She looked at the few dishes in the sink, mentally flipped a coin, and turned away from them. She dried Corsair and fed him, then let Bucephalus back in and dried and fed him. Gypsy ignored the dishes. Again.

Restlessly she took a long shower, changing the water from hot to cold halfway through and musing irritably over the untruth of certain remedies. She killed time by washing her hair, then stood naked in front of the vanity in the bathroom as she dried it with her dryer.

She stood there for a long moment after

the buzz of the dryer died into silence, staring into her own eyes. Resolutely she mentally flipped another coin.

The gown was in the bottom drawer of her dresser — just where Rebecca had placed it on one of her visits.

"You might need it, darling."

"I have the only mother on the West Coast who advises her daughter to go out and seduce a man."

"Surely not. Look at the statistics."

Silently Gypsy slipped the gown over her head. It was white silk, nearly transparent, and as form-fitting as a loving hand. Delicate lace straps were almost an afterthought to hold up the plunging V neckline. The silk was gathered slightly just beneath the V, then fell in a cascade of filmy material to her feet.

The matching peignoir was long-sleeved, made of see-through lace to the waist and silk from waist to floor. It tied in a little satin bow just at the V of the gown.

Gypsy slipped on the high-heeled mules and studied herself in the dresser mirror, a bit startled. Normally she wore a T-shirt to bed; seductive silk nightgowns had never been a part of her wardrobe. This one suited her, however. The stark whiteness emphasized her creamy tan and raven's-wing hair, and turned her eyes almost silver. Almost.

She scrabbled through three drawers to find the bottle of Christmas perfume never opened, locating it finally and using only a drop at the gown's V neckline.

"I'm going to feel like an absolute fool if this doesn't work out," she muttered to herself, leaving her bedroom after a hurried glance at the clock. It was just after midnight, and she didn't want to be around if her "night lover" decided to call tonight.

She left the pets in the kitchen, closing the back door behind her but not locking it. Who knew when she'd be back? She stood on the porch for a few moments, gazing over at Chase's house; only a few dim lights were on. Gypsy stepped off the porch . . . and her courage deserted her.

Only half aware that her high heels were sinking into the wet ground with every step, Gypsy began to pace back and forth. She held up the long skirt as she walked, absently addressing whatever shrub or flowering plant happened to be handy.

"*Now* what? Do I go over and ask to borrow a cup of sugar? In this outfit? Not exactly subtle, Gypsy. Why don't you just hit the man over the head with a two-by-four?"

She frowned fiercely at an inoffensive

holly bush. "So what if he rejects you? You're a big girl — relatively speaking. You can handle it. The world won't come crashing down around your ears if the man laughs at you. Will it?"

Since the holly bush remained mute, she paced on. A rosebush listened meekly to her next strictures.

"You're a grown woman, dammit! Why don't you act like one? You're only *technically* innocent, after all. You've probably seen things he's never seen! Why, you spent an entire summer observing the D.C. plainclothes cops, and if *that* didn't show you life, I don't know what would!"

The rose didn't venture a response, so Gypsy started to turn away. But she nearly fell. Regaining her balance, she looked down slowly. She was standing completely flat-footed: both heels had sunk completely into the wet earth.

Using words her mother had never taught her, Gypsy stepped out of the shoes. Still holding her skirt up, she bent over, wrestled the shoes from the clinging ground, and flung them angrily toward the house.

"A grown woman," she muttered derisively. "Just call me Pauline!"

Courage totally gone and ruefully aware that she couldn't pull off a seduction even if somebody drew her a diagram, Gypsy abandoned the idea. It would have to be up to Chase, she decided. And if she'd said "No involvement!" one time too many, then that, as the man said, was that.

Miserably wide-awake, Gypsy finally headed for the stairs leading down to the beach. Why waste her outfit? Let the moon have a thrill.

It was unusually warm for early June, and she briefly debated a moonlight swim before discarding the notion. It wasn't all that warm. And she didn't feel like swimming. She felt like sitting on her rock and crying for an hour or two. Or three.

Blind to everything except inner misery, she made for her rock as soon as the stairs had been successfully negotiated. But normal vision took over when she reached the rock. There was a white towel lying on it.

Gypsy picked up the towel slowly, blankly. Had someone left it here, or — Chase! Swimming alone? She turned quickly toward the roaring ocean, a sudden fear filling her sickeningly. It drained away in waves of relief as she saw him.

The huge orange moon, hanging low in the sky, silhouetted his head and shoulders as he moved toward the beach. Gypsy watched, hypnotized by the unforgettable sight of him rising from the ocean as raw as nature had made him.

He was all wild, primitive grace, curiously restrained power, she thought. His wet flesh glistened in the moonlight; rippling muscles were highlighted, shadowed. It was as if the Creator had begun with a jungle cat and then decided to mold a man instead from the living flesh. He was bold and strong and male, Gypsy felt — a living portrait of what a man could be. And Gypsy's heart nearly stopped beating.

She fixed her eyes on his shadowed face as he stopped before her, automatically handing him the towel with nerveless fingers. "You shouldn't swim alone," she said, wondering at the calm tone.

"I know." His voice was husky. He slowly knotted the towel around his lean waist.

Gypsy tried in vain to read his expression; the moon behind him prevented it. "Why did you?"

"I flipped a coin. Swimming won over a cold shower."

"They don't work, you know." She laughed shakily. "Cold showers, I mean."

"Have you tried?" he murmured, one hand lifting to brush a curl from her forehead.

She nodded. "Tonight. It didn't help."

His hand moved slowly downward, the knuckles lightly brushing along the plunging V of her gown until he was toying with the little satin bow. "And . . . you were coming to me, Gypsy mine?"

Gypsy swallowed hard, mentally burning her bridges. "I — I was. But I lost my courage."

"Why?"

He was nearer now, and she could see the catlike gleam of his jade eyes in the shadowy face. What was he thinking? "Because . . . I was afraid. Afraid you'd laugh at me."

"*With* you, yes. At you, never." His voice matched the muted roar of the ocean in its infinite certainty. His fingers abandoned the bow to slide slowly around her waist, his free hand lifting to cradle her neck. "You're so lovely. I thought I'd dreamed you. And now I'm afraid I'll wake up."

Gypsy felt damp, hair-roughened flesh against her palms, aware only then that she'd lifted her hands to touch his muscular chest. The pounding of the surf entered her bloodstream; the moonlight blinded her to reason. "If you wake up," she breathed, "wake me up too."

Chase made a soft, rough sound deep in his throat, bending his head to kiss her with a curiously fervent hunger. She could feel the restraint in his taut muscles, the fierce desire he couldn't hide, and a fire ignited somewhere deep in her inner being. Her arms slid up around his neck as Chase crushed her against his hard length, and Gypsy gloried in the strength of his embrace.

She met the seductive invasion of his tongue fiercely, her fingers thrusting through his thick hair and her body molding itself to his. Hunger ate at her like a starving beast, stronger than anything she'd ever known before.

In a single blinding moment of understanding, of clarity, she realized why she was taking this chance, why she was willing to risk pain. It was simply because she had no choice. This — whatever it was — was stronger, far stronger, than she was.

Chase lifted his head at last, breathing roughly, harshly. She could feel his heart pounding against her with the same untamed rhythm of her own. Staring up at him with dazed eyes, she realized that she was trembling, and that he was too.

"Let me love you, Gypsy mine," he pleaded thickly. "I need you so badly, so desperately . . ."

It wasn't in Gypsy to refuse, to protest. It just wasn't in her, she realized. She tightened her arms around his neck, rising up on tiptoe to press shaking lips to his, telling him huskily, "I thought you'd never ask. . . ."

He kissed her swiftly and then swung her up easily into his arms, heading across to the stairs leading up to his backyard. Surprisingly he chuckled softly. "I wouldn't dare try making love to you on the beach, sweetheart," he murmured whimsically. "One of us would be bound to get bitten by a sand crab . . . or something."

Gypsy found herself smiling. "Just call me Pauline."

"I'd rather call you mine." His arms tightened as he climbed the stairs, her slight weight obviously not bothering him in the least. "Fair warning. . . . I'm playing for keeps." He stopped at the top of the stairs, looking down at her as if waiting for her to change her mind . . . or to commit herself.

She fought back a sudden unease. "Can we talk about that tomorrow?" she asked softly, her lips feathering along his jawline.

"I'm not sure." His voice had grown hoarse. "I think I should have it in writing with you, sweetheart. You're so . . . damn . . . elusive!"

"Not really," she murmured, fascinated by the salty taste of his skin. "But if you keep standing here, it's going to start raining or something, and ruin the mood. . . ."

Rather hastily Chase headed for the deck. "You're so right, Pauline!"

Gypsy laughed, but her laugh faded away as he carried her through the glassed-in half of the deck to the sliding glass doors leading to his bedroom. The doors were open, and he brushed aside the gauzy drapes and carried her inside.

His bedroom was lighted only by a dim lamp on the nightstand. The covers were thrown back on the king-size bed, evidence of his inability to sleep. The room was definitely a man's room: solid, heavy oak furniture, earth tones — a place for everything and everything in its place. But there was a curious sensitivity in the unusual seascapes on the walls; they were lonely, bleak, riveting in their otherworldly aloneness.

Gypsy noticed little of the room; her full attention was focused on Chase. She could see his face clearly now in the lamplight, and the undisguised need gleaming in his jade eyes held her spellbound. She'd never seen such a look in a man's eyes before, and it made her suddenly, achingly aware of the hollow emptiness inside herself.

He set her gently on her feet beside the bed, his fingers lifting to fumble at the little satin bow. "Gypsy . . . I want you to be sure," he said roughly, as if the words were forced from him.

Shrugging off the lacy peignoir, she said unsteadily, "The only thing I'm sure of is that I'm glad I found you on the beach tonight."

His eyes darkening almost to black, Chase bent his head to touch his lips to hers as if she were something infinitely precious. His hands brushed the lacy straps of her gown off her shoulders, and Gypsy felt the cool slide of silk against her flesh as the gown fell to the deep pile of the carpeted floor. Her arms slid up around his neck, the searing shock of flesh meeting flesh sending tremors through her body as he crushed her against him.

His hands moved up and down her spine, pressing her even nearer, his mouth exploring hers as if he could never get enough of her. Tongues clashed in near-violent hunger as Gypsy matched his need with her own. She lost herself in that moment, something primitive possessing her with the strength of a fury.

Gypsy felt she wasn't close enough to him, could never be close enough, and the realization was maddening. She fumbled with the towel at his waist, flung it aside, just before he lifted her into his arms, placed her gently on the bed and came down beside her. Gypsy looked up at him, her eyes heavy with desire, watching as his gaze moved slowly over her body.

"So perfect," he murmured huskily. "So tiny and perfect. . . ." He bent his head, capturing the hardened tip of one breast with fervent lips.

Her senses spiraled crazily as his hands and lips explored. She was floating, being pulled inexorably in a single direction, and the current was too strong to resist. She felt the sensual abrasiveness of his hands, the heated touch of his mouth, and moved restlessly in a vain effort to ease the tormenting ache inside her.

"Gypsy. . . ." He rained kisses over her face, her throat; he took her hand and placed it on his chest. "Touch me, sweetheart. I need your touch. . . ."

Eagerly, driven by curiosity, by a starving sense of not knowing enough of him, she touched, explored. She felt the thick mat of dark gold hair curling on his chest, the muscles bunching and rippling with every move. Her fingers molded wide shoulders, traced along his spine, slid around to marvel at his flat, taut belly.

"I didn't know," she whispered, almost to herself.

"What?" he breathed, his mouth slowly trailing fire along a path leading him downward. The sensitive skin of her lower stomach quivered at the touch.

Gypsy gripped his shoulders fiercely, biting back a soft moan. "That a man could be so beautiful," she gasped.

"*You're* beautiful," he rasped softly, his fingers probing gently, erotically, until they found the heated center of her desire. "So sweet, Gypsy mine. . . ."

She was only dimly aware of her nails digging into his flesh, her eyes wide and startled at sensations she'd never experienced before. A strange tension grew within her, winding tighter and tighter until there was no bearing it. "Chase. . . ." she pleaded hurriedly, desperate to reach some unknown place, frantic to tap the critical mass building inside her frail body.

"Yes, darling. . . ." He rose above her, his breathing as rough and shallow as hers, eyes blazing darkly out of a taut face. With almost superhuman control he moved gently, sensitively.

Gypsy knew that he was being careful, trying not to hurt her. But the primitive fury possessing her burst its bounds, escaping with the exploding suddenness of a Pacific storm. She took fire in his arms, as wild as all unreason, giving of herself with passionate, innocent simplicity. She drew him deep inside herself fiercely, caught him in the silken trap of woman unleashed, held him with every fiber of her being. He was hers. For one brief, eternal moment he was hers, and she branded him. . . .

Gypsy barely stirred when Chase drew the sheet over their cooling bodies. Nothing short of a massive earthquake would have budged her from his side, and she didn't care how obvious that fact was to him. She felt drained, contented, and very much at peace.

"Gypsy?" He was raised on one elbow, gazing down at her with a sort of wonder in his eyes.

She looked up at him, smiling, much the same wonder shining in her eyes. Without thought she lifted a hand to touch his cheek, her smile turning misty when he held the hand with his own and gently kissed the palm.

"Rockets," he murmured whimsically, smiling crookedly at her. "And bells . . . and shooting stars . . . and earthquakes."

"You're welcome," she told him solemnly,

174

reaching for humor because she felt the moment was almost unbearably sweet.

Chuckling, he drew her even closer, arranging her at his side and wrapping his arms around her. "You're quite a lady, Gypsy mine."

She decided that his shoulder had been expressly designed for pillowing her head. "Well . . . I wasn't such a total slouch as a seductress after all, was I?"

"Honey," he laughed softly, "you've been seducing me since the day we met."

"Have I? Then why did you keep on talking about seducing *me?*"

"Encouraging you. I thought it was time you — uh — spread your wings."

"That was big of you."

"I thought so. After all — I'm a great supporter of the quest for human knowledge. And experience."

"Will you give me a reference?"

"Not a chance. We'll keep all your experience in the family."

"In the family?"

"No summer flings, Gypsy mine. I warned you. For keeps."

Gypsy was silent for a long moment. It warmed her that Chase should be so set on making a commitment, but it also disturbed her.

"Gypsy?" There was a thread of anxiety in his deep voice.

"You don't know what I'm like," she said softly. "You really don't know, Chase. I'm afraid . . . afraid I'll ruin things."

"Your writing?"

She nodded mutely, staring across the lamplit room at one of the lonely seascapes and wondering suddenly if there was a very lonely man behind Chase's cheerful facade.

"We can work it out, honey," he told her in a voice of quiet certainty. "I know we can. If you'll just give us a chance."

"How will you feel," she persisted tonelessly, "when I start ignoring you — maybe for days at a time? When I can't stand to be touched or bothered in any way? When I snap at you for no good reason? When I work around the clock?"

"We'll work it out," he repeated quietly.

"But what if we can't?" Her voice sounded afraid of itself.

"If we both make an effort, there's nothing we can't do. I promise you, sweetheart."

"I need time," she whispered. "Time to be sure." After a moment she felt his lips moving against her forehead.

"Then we'll take all the time you need." His hands began wandering beneath the covers, and he abruptly lightened the mood.

"Meanwhile back at the farm . . ."

"Chase . . ." She swallowed a giggle, wondering how he could have her near tears one moment and giggling the next.

"I'm hooked on you, Gypsy mine; you'll just have to accept that."

"Take your hand off my derriere, sir!" she commanded with injured dignity. "Or I shall retaliate!"

"Please do," he invited politely.

Luckily she just happened to discover his weakness. She tickled him and was immediately rewarded when he choked back a laugh.

"Gypsy —"

"Ha! You're ticklish! I knew there was a chink in the armor."

"I'm bigger than you, sweetheart," he warned, struggling to keep her hands away from ticklish places.

"Not if you're ticklish." Gypsy feinted and lunged with happy abandon, breaking through his defenses from time to time. "If you're ticklish, you're at my mercy!"

"Stop that, you witch!" He choked, making a vain attempt to pin her down to the bed. "I'll tickle you until you can't breathe," he promised threateningly.

"Go ahead." Gypsy launched another sneak attack, smiling with evil enjoyment.

177

"I'm not ticklish."

"What?" He looked horrified. "Not at all?"

"Well . . . there is *one* place."

"I'll find it," he vowed determinedly, hastily blocking her newest line of attack. "If it takes me the rest of my life!"

"Until then —" She commenced a two-handed, hell-for-leather attack.

"Gypsy!"

EIGHT

"Chase, you can't *do* that in a Jacuzzi."

"Says who?"

"Me. We'll drown."

"It's a chance in a million. I'm willing to risk it; how about you?"

"I have to get out. It's nearly noon. We've wasted the entire morning."

"Wasted?"

"Well . . ."

"You look so lovely . . . like Circe, rising from —"

"I hope you've got your legends mixed up," she interrupted tartly.

Chase was suspiciously innocent. "Why?"

"Circe turned men into swine, *that's* why."

"Sorry. Who do I mean?"

"I haven't the faintest idea."

"Helen of Troy?"

" 'The face that launched a thousand ships'? I don't look that good, pal."

"You launched my ship," he pointed out.

"It's not hard to launch a leaky canoe."

"I'll get you for that!"

"Chase! Stop it this instant! I'll tickle you! I swear, I —"

There was a long silence, broken only by the bubbling water, and then Gypsy's voice, bemused and breathless.

"Well, what do you know . . . you *can* do that in a Jacuzzi."

Chase headed into Portland after lunch to return their costumes, leaving Gypsy hard at work behind the typewriter. Half expecting to be dreamy-eyed and thoughtful after their first night together, she was more than a little surprised to find that she was able to keep her mind on writing. In fact, she turned out page after page that more than satisfied her own critical standards.

It was enough to spark a faint hope. If, somehow, Chase stirred her to write *better,* then perhaps the obsessions were a thing of the past. At least she could hope they were.

Daisy was delivered around four, and Gypsy was walking in a slow circle around the car when Chase pulled into the drive and began unloading the Mercedes.

"Groceries," he announced cheerfully. "Both our cupboards are bare. I see Daisy arrived safe and sound."

180

Gypsy automatically accepted the bag he handed to her. "Chase, you had her painted. And *all* the dents are out — not just the ones from the Mercedes."

"Looks pretty good, doesn't she?" Chase studied the little blue car critically. "I told them to reapply the daisy decals."

Still staring at him, Gypsy protested, "But she's got a whole new interior. New carpet, newly upholstered seats. Chase, the insurance didn't pay for all of that."

"Daisy deserves the best." He kissed Gypsy on the nose and headed for the house.

"Why?" Gypsy asked blankly, following behind. "And why haven't you had the dent taken out of the Mercedes? It's a *sin* to drive a dented Mercedes."

"The dent is a memento," he told her gravely, unloading the groceries in the kitchen. "And Daisy deserves the best because she introduced us. We probably wouldn't have met otherwise; until you came along, I never paid attention to neighbors."

"Oh." Gypsy thought that over for a while. "I hope you like lobster."

"Love it. You're *never* going to get the dent taken out?"

"That Mercedes will go to its grave with

181

the dent."

Gypsy helped Chase put away groceries. "I bet Freud could have had a field day with that," she murmured finally.

"I wouldn't doubt it. Through for the day?"

She blinked, remembered her writing, and nodded. "With the book. But I got a set of galleys in the mail, and I have to proof them. They have to go back in the mail tomorrow."

"Without fail?"

"Without fail."

"How long will it take you to proof them?"

"Couple of hours. Give or take."

"Ah! Then we'll have plenty of time."

"Time for what?" she asked innocently.

"To cook lobster, of course," he replied, totally deadpan.

"Let a girl down, why don't you."

"Never."

"Besides, I don't cook. Remember?"

"I'll cook. You'll keep me company. What is this?" He was holding up a covered plastic bowl taken from the refrigerator.

Gypsy crossed her arms and leaned back against the counter. "I don't remember what it started out to be. Now it's a whatisit."

"Come again?"

"A whatisit." She smiled gently at his bafflement.

"Is it alive?" he wondered, prudently not lifting the lid to find out.

"Probably." Gypsy choked back a giggle. "I warned you that I wasn't a housekeeper."

"I seem to remember that you did." Chase stared at the mysterious bowl for a moment, then placed it back in the refrigerator.

"Lack of courage?" she queried mockingly.

"Common sense. No telling how long that thing's been growing in there; it might bite by now."

"Superman would have looked."

"Superman would have thrown it into outer space."

Gypsy sighed mournfully. "They just don't make heroes like they used to."

"Pity, isn't it?" He lifted an eyebrow at her.

She crossed the room suddenly and wrapped her arms around his waist, hugging fiercely.

"Hey!" He was surprised, but clearly pleased. "What did I do?"

"You made Daisy beautiful." She hugged harder, rubbing her cheek against his chest. "Thank you."

"Superman would have gotten you a new

Daisy," he said gruffly, returning the hug with interest.

"Superman wouldn't have known I wanted *my* Daisy. You did."

"I won out over Superman?" he asked hopefully.

"Hands down. Let Lois have him."

Chase turned her face up gently, gazing down into misty gray eyes. "I think the lobster will wait awhile," he murmured.

"Lobsters are tactful souls. . . ."

Gypsy didn't get around to proofing the galleys until nearly midnight. And she only managed to get started then because she flatly refused to share Chase's shower.

"You'll be sorry. . . ."

"And you're a menace!" Gypsy carelessly discarded the caftan she'd been wearing all evening and climbed into bed. Ignoring her audience, she pulled the covers up, arranged them neatly, and drew the galleys forward. "I absolutely *have* to read these. Go take your shower."

There was a moment of silence, and then Chase said in a laughing voice, "I'd much rather watch you."

Gypsy was hanging half out of bed, fumbling beneath it and muttering to herself. "Ah!" She righted herself, rescued the sliding galleys, and held up a pair of her reading glasses in one triumphant hand. "I knew they were there somewhere."

"You keep a pair under the bed?" Chase asked politely.

"Where do —"

"I know," he interrupted ruefully. "Where do *I* keep glasses?"

"Am I in a rut?" she wondered innocently.

"No, sweetheart." He bent over the bed to kiss her lightly. "You're the last person in the *world* who could ever be in a rut."

"Close the door," she called after him, polishing her glasses on the sheet. "I don't need steamy galleys."

"If it's *steamy* you want —"

"Don't say it!"

The closing bathroom door cut off his laugh.

Smiling to herself, Gypsy began to read the galleys. She was vaguely aware of the shower going on in the bathroom, but concentrated completely on the job at hand. Until the phone rang.

Gypsy quickly picked up the receiver, only half her mind on the action. "Hello?"

"You were gone again last night."

She cast a baffled, harassed look toward the bathroom door. Dammit, it *had* to be Chase. "I told you to stop calling me!" she said fiercely.

" 'I am two fools, I know, for loving, and for saying so,' " he breathed sadly.

He was quoting Donne again.

Gypsy pushed the glasses to the top of her head and tried to think. "Don't call me again — and I mean it this time!"

"I dream of you," he whispered. "I dream of a voice like honey, of sweetness and gentleness. I believe in unicorns and heroes, and I wish on stars."

"Quit it," she said weakly.

"I created a dream-love, and she's you. She's the first flower of spring, the first star at night, the sun's first ray in the morning. She's a song I can't forget, a light in the darkness, and I love her."

"*Please,* quit it," Gypsy moaned desperately.

"Dream of me, love." The phone clicked softly.

Gypsy cradled the receiver. She nudged Corsair off her foot, not even noticing when he immediately resumed his favorite sleeping place. Undecided, she looked toward the bathroom door, then shook her head.

"No," she murmured to Corsair, or to Bucephalus beside the bed. "If I went and looked, he'd be there. And I don't think I could take it." She gazed into Corsair's china-blue eyes bemusedly. "I might well be in love with two men — and one of them's faceless, nameless, and probably a nut!"

When Chase came out of the bathroom a few minutes later, she was chewing on the earpiece of her glasses and staring into space.

Chase, a towel knotted around his waist, came over to the bed. He picked up Corsair, got Bucephalus by the collar, and escorted both to the door, shutting them out in the hall. When he turned around, he looked at Gypsy for a moment, then asked politely, "You'd rather they slept in here?"

"Hmmm?" She blinked at him.

"The pets." He crossed to sit on the foot of the bed, adding, "You were frowning at me."

"Cheshire cat," she murmured absently.

It was his turn to blink. "Earth to Gypsy?"

She stirred, finally giving him her full attention. "I wasn't frowning at you — I was just frowning."

"Why?"

Gypsy looked at him for a moment. "Seemed the thing to do."

Chase gave up. He shed the towel and climbed into bed beside her. "About finished up?" he asked seductively.

"About at the end of my rope," she confided seriously.

He propped himself up on an elbow and stared at her for a long moment. "You're just full of cryptic comments tonight, Gypsy mine."

"Uh-huh." Gypsy dumped the galleys on the floor beside the bed, dropping her glasses on top of them. "I'll do these in the morning. *Early* in the morning before the mailman comes. Don't let me forget."

"Perish the thought. . . ."

The galleys were late.

The next few days were interesting to say the least. Nights were alternately spent in Chase's house or Gypsy's, although days were generally spent at Gypsy's since she flatly refused to "clutter up" Chase's lovely den or study with her stuff.

She worked during the day; her story was still shaping without an obsessive urge to work constantly. Chase made several trips into Portland, where his office was located; he was officially on vacation, but since his was a one-man office, and since he was designing a house for Jake and Sarah, the trips were necessary.

But he was usually somewhere nearby. Gypsy would look up occasionally to see him stretched out on the couch reading, or hear him whistling in the kitchen. And he always made sure she ate regularly.

"I'll gain ten pounds if this keeps up!"

"Ten pounds on you would just be necessary ballast."

"Funny man. That 'ballast' won't be able to fit into my jeans."

"Have another roll."

With Chase, every day — and certainly every night — became an adventure. Gypsy never knew what he'd do next.

"What *is* that?"

"The mating call of whales."

"Really? I didn't even know you had an aquarium."

"Cute. It's a record. To set the mood."

"And I thought we were doing so well."

"Change is the spice of life, Gypsy mine."

"Right. Where's the water bed?"

"Damn. Knew I forgot something."

Gypsy discovered that it was definitely nice to have a man around. She was as mechanically inept as she was forgetful, her usual method of fixing anything being a few swift kicks or thumps.

"Chase, where are you?"

"In the kitchen feeding your pets."

She headed for the kitchen, announcing without preamble, "Herman's *e* is sticking, and it's driving me crazy. Can you do anything?"

Chase nearly lost a finger since he was giving Bucephalus a steak bone and looked up at the crucial moment. He stared at Gypsy for a second, then apparently deduced that Herman was the typewriter. "I'll certainly try," he told her, accepting named typewriters without a blink.

Ten minutes later Gypsy was happily typing again. "My hero," she murmured absently as Chase straightened from his leaning position against the desk. He touched her cheek lightly and said, "That's all I ever wanted to be, sweetheart."

Gypsy looked up only when he'd left the room. She stared after him for a long time, eyes distant and thoughtful. Then she bent her head and went back to work.

Chase came in late one afternoon to find her pounding the keys furiously and wearing a fierce grimace that didn't invite interruption.

"Gypsy —"

"Hush!" she said distractedly, hammering away at her top speed, which was pretty impressive. "Someone's about to get killed."

It was half an hour before her assault on Herman ceased. Gypsy straightened and rubbed the small of her back absently, reading over what she'd written. Only then did she become aware of a presence. She looked up to find Chase leaning against the book-case and watching her with a faint smile.

"Hello," she said in surprise. "How long have you been there?"

"A few minutes. I tried to interrupt you, and you told me to hush."

"Oh, I'm sorry," she muttered, horrified.

He chuckled softly. "Don't be. I knew it was the wrong time but, to be honest, I wanted to find out what you'd do. And if that was the worst, we're home free, sweet-heart."

Gypsy pushed her glasses up on top of her head, never noticing that the pair already there fell to the floor behind her. She looked curiously at his trying-hard-to-hide grin. "We'll have to wait and see, won't we?" she murmured in response to his com-ment.

"If you say so. What would you like for dinner?"

Gypsy's "night lover" continued to call whenever she and Chase were spending the night in her house. Chase was always around, but never in the room, and her suspicions were growing by leaps and bounds. It was much easier, she admitted to

191

herself ruefully, to believe that it was Chase; otherwise, she was quite definitely in love with two separate men . . . and *there* was a wonderfully cheering thought!

A few days later, suddenly and with no warning, her book became an obsession. It wasn't too bad at first; Chase found wonderfully unique ways of getting her away from the typewriter for a break or a meal or sleep — and all without causing her to lose her temper once.

"Gypsy?"

"Not now."

"You have to help me — it's desperately important!"

"What then?"

"My zipper's stuck."

"Chase!"

"It got you away from the typewriter."

"I know, but really!"

"Now that you're *here* —"

"You're incorrigible!"

Or:

"Gypsy?"

"What?"

"You have to help me."

"What's desperately important now?"

"I have to get my car keys."

"Chase, you've been up that tree every morning for weeks; you should know the way by now."

"Corsair went up a different tree. Sneaky cat."

"I'll bet you told him to."

"How could I? He doesn't listen to me. Come now, Gypsy mine, just a moment of your time. I don't ask for much, after all."

"Stop sounding pitiful; it won't wash."

"It was worth a try."

He found her outside one morning, sitting cross-legged on the ground and methodically pulling up handfuls of grass.

"Why are you mangling the lawn?" he asked sweetly, sinking down beside her.

Gypsy was fixedly watching her hands. "I've painted myself into a corner, dammit," she muttered irritably. "And now I don't see . . ."

"Let the paint dry and repaint the room," he advised cheerfully, obviously without the least idea of what she was talking about.

She froze, lifting startled eyes to his. "Wait a minute. That just might work. I could — And then —" She reached over to hug him exuberantly. "You did it! Thank you!"

Chase followed her into the house, murmuring, "Great. What did I do?"

Chase managed to get her away from the typewriter all day the following Sunday by inviting her parents to have dinner and spend the afternoon at his house. Gypsy was inclined to be temperish about it at first; in fact, it was the first time she really snapped at him — and it upset her more than it did Chase.

"*Why* did you do that? I can't stop working for a whole day! I'll never get this book finished, dammit, and it's all your fault!"

"Gypsy —"

"You've messed up my whole life!"

"Have I?" he asked softly.

She stared at him and her anger vanished. Quickly she rose from her chair and went over to him, wrapping her arms around his waist. "Why do you put up with me?" she asked shakily.

"Well, you're just an occasional shrew," he told her conversationally. "And I always did prefer tangy to sweet."

"Chase —"

"Cheer up. You haven't seen *my* worst side yet."

"Do you have one? I was thinking of having you canonized."

"Saint Chase?" He tried the title on for size. "Doesn't sound right, somehow. We'll have to think it over. Come along now, Gypsy mine; we're going to prepare a feast for your parents."

"We?"

"This time you get to help."

"Help do what? Kill us all? Face it, pal —
I have absolutely no aptitude for cookery."

"You can slice things, can't you?"

"You're going to let me have a knife?"

"On second thought I'll do the slicing.
You can set the table and keep me company."

"As I asked once before, is your china
insured?"

"Since the day after I met you."

The entire day was fun laced with nonsense, and Gypsy thoroughly enjoyed it. She
always enjoyed her parents' visits, but
Chase's presence made it even better. He
got along very well with both of them, accepting Gypsy's definitely unusual parents
with clear enjoyment.

And they just as clearly approved of him:

"Mother, what were you and Chase in a
huddle about?"

"Nothing important, darling. Are you
working on a book? You don't look as tired
as usual."

Knowing her mother, Gypsy accepted the
change of subject. "Chase makes me rest."

"Your father is just the same with me.
When's the wedding?"

"Are you and Poppy getting married

again, Mother?"

"Gypsy . . ."

"He hasn't asked, Mother."

"Nonsense, darling. He doesn't have to."

"Etiquette demands it."

"Write a new rule. Ask him."

"I'm an old-fashioned kind of girl."

"Stubborn. Just like your father."

"Poppy, where are you going with that ladder?"

"Corsair stole *my* car keys. He's on the roof; Chase is going up after him."

"Oh. Chase had a ladder all this time? I'll get him for that; I've been helping him out of trees all week."

"Corsair?"

"Chase."

"Oh, I like him, darling."

"Corsair?"

"You're worse than your mother. Chase, of course."

"Stop smiling at me, Poppy."

"I like smiling at you; fathers do that, you know."

"Yes, but it's *that* kind of smile. A definitely parental Father-always-knows-kid-and-don't-try-to-hide-it kind of smile. Unnerving."

"You're misreading my expression. This is

my I-want-to-dandle-a-grandchild-on-my-knee-one-day smile."

"Poppy —"

"I'll take the ladder to Chase."

"Do that."

"Did you get Corsair off the roof?"

"After a merry chase, yes. Your cat has a devious mind."

"I've been meaning to tell you. If you'd only stop playing his game, he'd stop too. He never would have gone up a tree a second time if you'd only ignored him the first time."

"I needed my keys."

"He would have dropped them. Eventually."

"Uh-huh."

Days passed and Gypsy became more and more wrapped up in her book. The clutter on her desk, composed of notes on odd sheets of paper, reference books, and assorted alien objects like the Buddha, grew until it was nearly impossible to find her or Herman in the middle of it. Chase pulled her from the muddle for meals but otherwise left her strictly alone.

Gypsy made a tremendous effort and firmly stopped working at midnight every night. She'd never held herself to any kind of fixed schedule before, and was agreeably surprised to find that it didn't seem to be interfering with her creativity. If anything, it helped; she always stopped before she got too tired now.

Besides . . . she cherished the nights with Chase. He showed her an enchantment she had never before known, and she loved him more with every day that passed. Neither of them ever put their feelings into so many words, and she had a suspicion that Chase wouldn't say a word until she did. He'd said that he was "playing for keeps" and was leaving the rest up to her.

But Gypsy still wasn't ready to commit herself fully. She was still uneasy, still worried that his patience would run out.

And it did.

As the book neared its completion Gypsy warned him that the midnight halts were at an end. The last few days of a book were written in a white-hot headlong rush, interrupted by nothing except a catnap when the typewriter keys blurred before her eyes. At that point Gypsy was driven by the need to just *finish* the thing, and there was nothing else she could do.

It went on for three days. Gypsy ate little and rarely left her desk. She catnapped on the couch at odd hours, then took showers to refresh her mind before going immediately back to work. She was dimly aware of Chase, but not distracted by his presence. As for Chase, he was always around but didn't intrude.

Three days. At two a.m. on the fourth day, the headlong rush came to a crashing halt.

Gypsy found herself jerked suddenly to her feet, banging both knees against the desk's center drawer, and quite thoroughly and ruthlessly kissed.

"Do I have your attention now?" Chase demanded hoarsely.

She blinked up at him, a bit startled by the suddenly unleashed primitive man. Clearing her throat carefully, Gypsy barely managed a one-word response. "Yes."

"Good!" He lifted the glasses from her nose, dropped them on the foot-high clutter on the desk, and then threw Gypsy over his shoulder with one easy, lithe, far from gentle move.

"Chase!" Dangling helplessly, she realized that he was carrying her into the bedroom.

"*Don't* have me canonized!" he snapped.

"Chase, what're you —" She bounced once on the bed, looking up with wide eyes as he joined her with a force that stole her breath. "Chase?"

He kissed her with a roughness just this side of savagery, a bruising impatience that stripped away all the civilized layers of the mating game. His hunger was voracious, insatiable. Restraint was gone, gentleness was gone; there was only this crucial need, this desperate hunger.

Gypsy had believed that she could never be surprised by his lovemaking, but she discovered her mistake. And after the first moment of shock, she responded with a mindless need to match his own wild hunger.

It was silent and raw and indescribably powerful. They loved and fought like wild things compelled to mate once and die, their movements swift and hurried and uncontrolled. Something primal drove them relentlessly, pushing them higher and higher, until they soared over the brink in a heart-stopping, mind-shattering release. . . .

Floating in a dreamy haze, Gypsy was lying on her back close beside Chase. She felt his arm, heavy across her middle, heard his rough breathing gradually steady. She wanted to smile all over. Eyes closed, she felt rather than saw Chase raise himself on an elbow, felt his gaze.

"Honestly," she murmured in an injured tone, "you could have just asked, pal. I mean — I think they used to call it ravishment."

"Gypsy . . ."

Startled by his hesitant, anxious voice, her eyes snapped open. She looked up at him, searching his concerned face and darkened eyes, realizing in slow astonishment that he was really worried. She wasn't about to let *that* go on.

Sliding her arms up around his neck, she allowed her inner smile to show through. "You should get creative more often."

The jade eyes lightened, but he still looked anxious. "You really don't mind?" he asked in a low voice. "I didn't mean to be so rough, honey."

Gypsy rather pointedly traced a long scratch on his shoulder with one finger. "We both got a little carried away. Let's get carried away again . . . real soon."

He chuckled softly, apparently realizing that she wasn't the slightest bit upset by ravishment. "You should be mad, Gypsy mine; I interrupted your work."

"With a vengeance," she agreed dryly. "But I forgive you. I only had a few pages left to do anyway."

"To finish the book?" When she nodded, he said ruefully, "That close to the end and I stopped you. . . . You should be furious."

"No, but I am *curious*. What finally pushed you over the edge? I mean, you've been Saint Chase for weeks."

"I'm not quite sure." He paused, then went on firmly, "Yes, I am sure, dammit. I was jealous."

"Jealous?" Gypsy was startled. "Of what?"

"The book. The typewriter. The desk. Everything standing between you and me. I was lying here in bed — alone, I might add — and suddenly decided that enough was enough."

Gypsy frowned uneasily, and he immediately understood her worry.

"Honey, I really don't think that your writing will get between us. It only happened tonight because . . . because you're still so *new* to me." His voice deepened, roughened. "You're like a treasure I stumbled on by accident — I want to keep you to myself for a while. I want to — to hoard my riches until I'm sure I won't lose them."

She tried to speak past the lump in her throat, but found it impossible.

"Still . . ." He was suddenly rueful, obviously trying to lighten the atmosphere. "The White Knight wouldn't have approved."

Tightening her arms around his neck, Gypsy swallowed the lump and said huskily,

"The White Knight doesn't know what he's missing. And neither does his lady."

"Hey . . ." He smiled down at her. "I win out over the White Knight too?"

"He's not even in the same race."

Chase kissed her gently, murmuring, "You're running out of heroes, Gypsy mine."

"I hadn't noticed. . . ."

NINE

Due to one thing or another — and Chase fit into both categories — Gypsy didn't finish her book until late the next day. As always, the book was too fresh in her mind for her to be objective about it. She only knew that she was satisfied.

She woke the next morning with the disquieting sensation that something was wrong, and it took only seconds for her to realize what it was. Chase wasn't in bed with her. She listened to the silent house for a moment, then slid out of bed and put on one of his T-shirts. By this time both their wardrobes were pretty equally divided between the two houses.

She padded soundlessly through the house until she reached the doorway of the living room. There she stopped, leaning against the wall and watching him with quiet eyes.

He was sitting at her desk, the chair pushed back to accommodate his long legs.

Dressed only in cutoff jeans, hair still tousled from sleep, his head was bent over the last few pages of Gypsy's manuscript. He'd obviously been there for some time.

When he'd read the last page, Chase turned it facedown with the others in a stack on the corner of the desk, his expression thoughtful. He looked up suddenly a moment later, as though sensing her presence. Gazing at her, he murmured, "I think it's the best thing you've ever written."

Gypsy came across to him, sinking down on the carpet at his feet with her folded hands resting across his thigh. "Why?" she asked, her voice as soft as his in the early-morning hush.

Chase reached out to stroke her tumbled curls absently, frowning slightly in thought. "Certain things haven't changed — from your other books, I mean. It's ruthlessly logical, neatly plotted, with unexpected twists and turns. But your *characters* are different. Especially the hero." Chase smiled suddenly. "He's the type you want to stand up and cheer for. Not an *anti*hero like the others, but a human hero with strengths and weaknesses. He's smart but not cynical, idealistic without being a fool. And he has a fiendish sense of humor. You'll have to make him a continuing character, sweetheart —

readers will love him."

Gypsy smiled, more than content with the critique. "I'm glad you think it's good."

"It's more than good, Gypsy mine. It's terrific. A sure bestseller." He leaned forward to kiss her lightly, remaining in that position as he gazed into her eyes and asked casually, "Want to go to Virginia with me?"

"Virginia?" She was still smiling. "What's in Virginia?"

He seemed to hesitate for an instant. "A project they want me to do."

Her smile faded slightly. "They?"

"The city fathers in Richmond. The project I worked on for two months was for them. Now they want a big shopping mall."

Dimly Gypsy realized that it would be a professional feather in Chase's cap. "When do you have to be there?"

"I'm supposed to meet with them Friday afternoon."

"That's tomorrow," she said slowly. "How long — I mean, will you have to be there for months?"

"Not at this early stage. We'll be talking about budgets and designs — that sort of thing. Guidelines have to be ironed out before they commit themselves, and before I commit myself. It'll take days. Weeks, if they're as slow as last time."

He was still smiling, but there was a curiously blank look in his eyes, as if he were deliberately hiding his thoughts. "Come with me?"

"I can't."

"Jake and Sarah'll watch the houses for us." He was still casual.

She shook her head. "That's not it. The book's finished, Chase, but the manuscript isn't. I have days of retyping to do."

"I see." His eyes remained blank. "Can't type in Richmond, I guess?"

Gypsy felt strangely shaken by his light tone, disturbed by the shuttered gaze. "Would it be worth the bother to carry all my stuff out there?" she asked uncertainly. "You said it might just be days, and —"

"You're right, of course." He sat back, looking down at her with a glinting smile. "Then I go alone." Softly he added, "You're still not sure about us, are you, Gypsy?"

Before she could answer, he rose to his feet and pulled her gently to hers. "I'll catch an afternoon plane today; I'll need time to check out the proposed site tomorrow before the meeting. And since I have a few things to take care of in Portland before I leave — I'd better get a move on, I guess. Want to help me pack?"

"You're leaving right away?" she asked weakly.

"After breakfast. I'll cook if you'll pack for me. Deal?"

Two hours later he was gone, leaving Gypsy at the door with a light kiss and a cheerful wave.

His eyes had still been blank.

"Well, dammit. . . ." Gypsy muttered miserably to herself, watching the Mercedes disappear from sight.

Days passed, while Gypsy worked to retype her manuscript. She worked long hours, but not because the story drove her; she worked because something else was driving her.

Chase called every evening around eight to report progress (none, from the sound of it). He was casual, cheerful. He didn't once call her Gypsy mine or sweetheart or honey. He didn't talk about heroes.

So Gypsy threw herself into her work. She worked so fiercely that the manuscript was retyped and on its way to her editor by the middle of that week. And then she was at loose ends, struggling to find things to do. She gardened. She washed Daisy three times in two days. She used the key Chase had left her to let herself into his house and take care of Angel and the kittens. She watched television. She read poetry.

Poetry. If it hadn't been for her "night lover," Gypsy didn't know what she would have done. He called every night around midnight. Gypsy always listened intently, trying to pin down the voice, trying to convince herself it was Chase. But she just wasn't sure. And she was too fearful of a negative answer to ask if it was him.

" 'Come live with me and be my love,' " he invited softly one night.

Lying in bed in darkness, Gypsy smiled to herself. "Will you show me 'golden sands and crystal brooks'?" she murmured.

"I'll show you . . . the ones inside myself," he vowed. "I'll show you all the things you have to *believe* in before you can see them. Will you let me do that, love?"

She laughed unsteadily. "You haven't shown me *you.*"

"I'm one of those things that has to be believed first, love. If you believe in me, then I'm real."

"Like unicorns?" she whispered.

"Like unicorns. And heroes."

Gypsy tried desperately to deny the emotions welling up inside of her. "I can't believe in you," she told him shakily. "I —"

"You must believe in me, love. Without you I can't exist."

"Don't say that. . . ."

"Dream of me, love."

Gypsy found herself pacing the next night. Pacing restlessly, endlessly. She had talked to Chase only an hour before; a casual, meaningless conversation. Why was he doing this to her? He was deliberately holding back a part of himself, and —

She stopped dead in the center of the room, her lips twisting suddenly as the realization slammed at her. "Idiot!" she breathed softly to her usual audience of Corsair and Bucephalus. "Of course, that's what he's doing. He's showing you what it's like, you fool! You've spent weeks huddled inside your own stupid uncertainties, while he waited patiently for you to — to grow up."

What was she *really* afraid of? Gypsy asked herself. Not that they couldn't live together — they could. Not that her writing would come between them — because, dammit, she wouldn't let it.

"Drag out the cliché, Gypsy," she told herself softly. "You're really afraid of getting hurt. You told yourself for years that you didn't want to get involved, and when it finally happened, it scared you to death. For the first time in your life, you let someone

210

close enough to see you. And now . . . ?"

Facing the fear squarely for the first time, she realized slowly, gladly, that it was fading into nothingness. Chase would never hurt her — not intentionally. And being seen by him was a very special thing indeed. She only hoped that it wasn't too late to tell him.

Gypsy's heart thudded abruptly as a sudden painful question presented itself. It pounded in her head, slammed at walls already crumbling, leaving panic in its wake.

What if she lost him?

Not the vague, elusive worry of "someday," but the concrete realization that life was uncertain at best. What if he never came back? What if she never saw him again, was never given the chance to say . . .

One glance at the clock and Gypsy was sitting on the edge of her bed and reaching for the phone. It was midnight in the East; he'd be at his hotel. She placed the call and listened as his phone rang, her only thought that "tomorrow" was sometimes too late.

"Hello?"

"I miss you," she said starkly.

"Do you?" He was guarded, his voice still and waiting.

"Chase . . ."

"You sound upset." It was a question.

"I'm lonely." She laughed shakily. "For

211

the first time in my life, I'm lonely. Are you
— When are you coming home?"

He sighed. "Looks like another few days."

Gypsy closed her eyes, knuckles showing
white as she gripped the receiver. "I don't
think I can wait that long."

"Gypsy?"

"Nothing's right." Her voice was hurried,
half blocked by the lump in her throat.
"Nothing's the same. The house seems
empty. . . . Bucephalus isn't eating. . . . I
can't find my glasses. . . . The Buddha fell
off my desk, and he's shattered, just shattered. . . . Corsair goes from room to room,
and he can't seem to find what he's looking
for —"

"Gypsy —"

"Angel moved her kittens back to your
bedroom," she went on disjointedly. "And
some kind of bug's attacking the roses. I
washed dishes last night because I didn't
want to be messy, and I picked up all the
clothes on the floor. . . . It rained all day. . . .
My bed's so big . . . so empty. . . ."

"I'm catching the first plane home," he
told her, his voice oddly unsteady.

"But your work —"

"Never mind my work. You're more important. I'll be home tomorrow, honey."

"I'll be waiting," she promised huskily.

"Good night, Gypsy mine."

"Good night."

Gypsy cradled the receiver gently, staring across the room blindly.

"You're more important."

Her mind flashed back to an earlier inner resolution not to let her writing come between them, and she felt a sort of wonder. Somehow, without her being consciously aware of it, the two most important things in her life had softly changed places. From now on, she knew, nothing would ever be as important as Chase.

As for her writing . . . Gypsy shook her head ruefully. It had been right there in front of her all the time, and she'd never seen it. But Chase had. He'd told her that her fictional hero was "the kind you want to stand up and cheer for," and she hadn't realized the importance of that.

She could imagine heroes now. Human heroes; fallible, but heroes nonetheless. And Chase had given her that. Chase and her "night lover."

Gypsy frowned suddenly. It was Chase. Period. She'd go on playing the game as long as he did, and just stop questioning. And one day, when they were old and gray and rocking side by side on a vine-covered porch, she'd ask him. And if he didn't say yes . . . she'd hit him with her cane.

"Do you believe in unicorns, love."
  "Yes," she whispered.
  "And heroes?"
  "And heroes."
  "And . . . me?"
  "And you." Her voice was tender.
  "We'll find those 'golden sands and crystal brooks,' " he told her with impossible sweetness. "We'll follow rainbows until we find the pot of gold. And when it storms outside, when the world goes crazy, we'll have each other."
  "Never alone," she murmured wonderingly.
  "Never alone. Sweet dreams, love. . . ."

Gypsy was restless, on edge. She was bursting to tell Chase how she felt, and the morning dragged by with no sign of him. She washed Daisy again and cultivated two flower beds, and *still* he didn't come.

  She wandered around the house, trying to rehearse what she wanted to say. But she knew ruefully that — rehearsals notwithstanding — heaven only knew what would come out of her mouth when the moment came.

  It was after two when she finally left the

house, wandering out to the edge of the cliffs and sitting down on the grass at the top of the steps. She stared out over the ocean, her mind empty of everything except the wish that he would come to her.

She didn't hear him coming, but was instantly aware when he knelt on the grass just behind her.

"Gypsy?"

She twisted around abruptly, her arms going around his neck with blind certainty. She felt his arms holding her tightly, felt the smooth material of his shirt and the heavy beat of his heart beneath her cheek.

"I've found a new kind of hero," she told him breathlessly. "A kind I never knew existed."

"What kind?" he asked gently, holding her as if he would never let her go.

"He makes me laugh. And he doesn't mind that I'm messy and can't cook. He fixes Herman and helps me find my glasses and cooks marvelous meals for me. He makes me stop work to help him down from trees, even though he's got a ladder. He does impossible things in Jacuzzis and plays music made by whales, and thinks I'm a treasure he stumbled on by accident. He puts up with a huge dog and an invasion of cats, and keeps a dent in his Mercedes. And he's so very patient with me. . . ."

"Gypsy . . ." Chase turned her face up with gentle hands, looking down at her with glowing jade eyes.

"I love you," she told him fiercely. "I love you so much, and if you can only put up with me —"

"Put up with you?" His voice was an unsteady rasp. "God, Gypsy, don't you realize what you mean to me?" He rubbed his forehead against hers in a rough movement. "When we first met, I didn't know whether to kiss you or have you committed. Within six hours I knew that I wanted you committed — to me. For the rest of our lives. I love you, sweetheart."

"Chase . . ." Gypsy closed her eyes blissfully as his lips met hers. She was dimly aware of movement but was not troubled by it, responding with all the love inside herself to the sweetness of his kiss. When her lashes finally drifted open again, she discovered that she was lying on her back in the soft grass, with Chase lying close beside her. His lips were feathering lightly along her jawline, teasing the corner of her mouth.

"Why did you leave me?" she asked huskily, knowing the answer but needing to hear it from him. "Why were you so — so indifferent?"

"I was gambling, Gypsy mine," he murmured, lifting his head to gaze into her eyes. "You still weren't sure about us, and I was going crazy trying to think of some way of proving to you that we belonged together. So I decided to leave, suddenly and with little warning. I hoped you'd miss me. But driving away that morning was the hardest thing I've ever done in my life. These last days have been hell," he finished roughly.

Gypsy touched his cheek, a gentle apology for the pain of his uncertainty, and her senses flared when he turned his head to softly kiss her palm.

"Everything happened so fast that morning," she said. "You didn't give me a chance to stop and think; you were just gone."

His smile was twisted wryly. "If I'd given you a chance to think, honey, I would have given myself one as well. And I never would have gone. It was like taking bad-tasting medicine; I had to get it over with quickly."

"And . . . the project in Richmond?" she asked softly.

"Oh, it was real. They called me a couple of weeks before I left. The project's on, by the way. There are still a few details to be hammered out, but the contract's being drawn up now. Would you like to spend the winter in Richmond, Gypsy mine?"

217

"I've never been to Richmond." She smiled up at him, and then the smile turned wondering. "I just can't believe it," she said almost to herself. "I'm so hopeless to live with, and yet you —"

"Honey . . ." He shook his head with a faint smile, and went on slowly. "You brought something different into my life, something special. There aren't enough hours in the day for me now, because every one brings something new and exciting. Don't you realize how fascinating you are just to *watch?*"

He kissed her lightly on the nose, one finger tracing the curve of her cheek. "The way you blink like a startled kitten when you're surprised. The way you absentmindedly put on one pair of glasses while another's on the top of your head. The way you explain something totally ridiculous with all the reasonableness in the world.

"You accept the absurd without a blink and make the commonplace seem fascinating. You have a mind as sharp as a razor, and yet you can never find whatever you're looking for. You have a penchant for naming objects and talking to them — and about them — as if they were people. You're prone to collect strange things like Buddhas, and the urge to collect them honestly bewilders you." He smiled tenderly at her. "And when I'm with you, I feel as if I'm on the world's biggest roller coaster — exhilarated and breathless."

Gypsy tried to think straight. "But I can't cook, and I'm not a housekeeper."

He kissed her suddenly, as if he couldn't help himself, and she realized that he was laughing silently.

"How you do harp on that," he chided gently. "Do you think I give a damn that you don't cook and aren't a housekeeper? So what? I couldn't write a book if you took me through it sentence by sentence. I couldn't create a hero you'd want to stand up and cheer for —"

"Yes, you could," she interrupted breathlessly, the emotions inside of her threatening to burst their fragile human shell.

Chase hugged her silently, a suspicious shine in the jade eyes. "The point is," he went on huskily, "that I don't have to 'put up' with you at all, honey. I love everything about you. You're beautiful inside and out. Warm and giving, humorous and ridiculous, and passionate. You fill my days with laughter and my nights with magic. From the moment I saw compassion in your lovely eyes for the lonely little boy I might have been, I knew that I'd found the woman I've been looking for all my life. The treasure I stumbled on by accident . . ."

"I love you, Chase," she told him shakily. "I was so empty when you left, so alone. I realized then that if I never wrote another word, it wouldn't bother me — but if I never saw you again, I'd die. I was so stupid, so stupid not to see it sooner!"

"My love," he murmured, kissing her.

Long moments passed, the silence broken only by the muted roar of the ocean, the soft twittering of birds, and murmurs of love.

"I really hate to break the mood," Gypsy said at last, her voice grave, "but I think we'd better get up."

"Why?" he lifted a brow at her. "No neighbors."

"Neighbors are closer than you think." Gypsy made a slight, restless movement. "Uh . . . I believe you put me down on an ant's nest."

Chase began to laugh helplessly.

She grinned up at him. "Just call me Pauline!"

Still laughing, Chase got to his feet and helped her up. "I believe I've mentioned it before, sweetheart, but even Cyrano would have a hell of a time trying to romance you!"

"Are you glad you've got me instead?" she

asked politely.

"I can't believe my luck." He began enthusiastically brushing her down to remove possible ants.

"Chase?"

"What?"

"I was lying on my back. Not my front."

"So you were, so you were." He grinned at her, linking his hands together at the small of her back as they stood close together.

"You're impossible!" she told him severely.

"Can I help it if I can't keep my hands off you?" he asked, wounded.

"Dignity," she said austerely, "should be our uniform of the day."

"That uniform won't fit either one of us."

"We must strive to cultivate dignity," she insisted solemnly.

"Why?"

"Because we're grown-up adult people, that's why."

"Are we?" Chase frowned thoughtfully. "I don't think so."

"We'd better be, if we're going to get married. Are we going to get married?"

"Of course we are."

"I wondered. You never said."

"I was waiting for you to ask me."

Gypsy thought of her mother's advice, and

bit back a giggle. "Never let it be said that I didn't do what was expected of me. Shall I make an honest man out of you? I think I shall. Will you marry me?"

"You're supposed to get down on your knees and swear undying love," he pointed out critically.

"Can't I stand and swear undying love?" she asked anxiously. "The ants, you know."

"I'm willing to stretch a point," he allowed graciously.

"Thank you." Gypsy tightened her arms around his neck and looked up at him soulfully. "My darling, you're everything I didn't dare hope to find, everything I looked for in my dreams." The light mockery fell away from her slowly as she gazed at the lean face that meant so much to her.

"I can face the worst of life with you beside me, and enjoy the best of life as I never would without you. I'd do anything for you, pay any price for your love. I'd willingly give up everything that ever mattered to me if you asked it of me. I'd follow you through the fires of hell itself." Her voice became suddenly unsteady, but not uncertain. "I'll love you until I die . . . and after. Will you marry me, my love?"

Chase drew a deep, shuddering breath, his arms tightening fiercely around her.

"Yes, please," he said simply.

Gypsy swallowed the lump in her throat and smiled tremulously up at him. "Now we're betrothed," she said gravely.

"And a very short betrothal it'll be, love," he told her firmly. "I hope you hadn't planned on a big wedding."

"What? With my *Perils of Pauline* luck?" Gypsy was honestly horrified. "I wouldn't dare! I'd trip over my train, or drop the flowers — or the ring —"

Chase was laughing. "You probably would, Gypsy mine. So we'll have a nice quiet wedding as soon as it can be arranged. Would your parents mind if we were married at the office of a justice of the peace?" A whimsical expression crossed his face as he thought of Gypsy's parents. "Stupid question," he murmured.

Gypsy was grinning up at him. "My parents wouldn't mind if we were married in the middle of Portland during rush hour — just as long as it's legal."

"Mmmm." Chase lifted an eyebrow. "Dad won't be able to get leave to return to the States for the wedding, so you'd better be prepared for a second ceremony — in Switzerland."

"Switzerland?" she mumbled.

"Uh-huh. Nice place for a honeymoon,

don't you think? I can watch you wrap Dad around your little finger, and then we can spend a few weeks seeing all the places the tourists miss. We'll even rent a chalet — that way we won't have to bother about DO NOT DISTURB signs. How does that sound?"

Gypsy frowned at him. "Why do I suddenly get the feeling that you've had this arranged for quite a while?"

Chase looked thoughtful, the jade laughter in his eyes giving him away. "I couldn't say — unless it's because you know me so well, sweetheart."

"Chase!"

He chuckled softly. "Guilty — and I don't regret it a bit. Actually I called Dad during one of those hellish nights in Richmond and told him that I was bringing my bride to the Alps as soon as possible, and would he please rent a chalet for us?" Chase looked reflective. "I'm sure I sounded a little wild. Anyway Dad can't wait to meet you."

Gypsy realized that her mouth was open, and hastily closed it. "Oh, Lord," she murmured.

"He already knows you from your books," Chase was going on cheerfully. "We share an addiction for mysteries. As a matter of fact, we both agree that you're number one; we each have your books hardbound, and guard them jealously."

"You never told me that," she mumbled, suddenly remembering Jake's comment about Chase's "raving" over her books.

"You never asked." He kissed her nose; it seemed to be a favorite spot for him. "How many children shall we have, Gypsy mine?"

She blinked. "You like your questions loaded, don't you?"

"Never answer a question with a question," he chided gravely. "I was thinking of three. That's a nice, uneven number. However, I absolutely *insist* on being consulted over the names. Otherwise, our children will end up with names like Vladimir or Shadwell or Zenobia or Radinka. Or Bucephalus."

"I didn't name him!" Gypsy objected, trying not to laugh.

"I have my suspicions about that," Chase told her darkly.

Gypsy giggled, and then sobered. "Three," she murmured, and then looked up at Chase with sudden vulnerability and uncertainty in her eyes. "Our children. . . . Darling, I'd love to be a mother, but do you think —"

He laid a gentle finger across her lips, cutting off doubts. "Our children will cherish their mother all the days of their lives," he assured her huskily. "They'll come to her with their laughter and their tears, because she'll laugh with them and cry with them. She'll be the type of mother who'll gather all the neighborhood kids at her house for an impromptu party or a picnic, and she'll never run out of games or stories. It'll be a disorganized home, filled with laughter and love, and innumerable pets — and I wouldn't miss it for the world!"

After a moment of drowning in the warm jade depths of his eyes, Gypsy murmured softly, "In that case, three won't be enough."

He kissed her nose again. "I'm open to negotiations, darling."

"Why don't we try out that Jacuzzi of yours again?" she suggested solemnly. "It should be a good place to . . . negotiate."

"Great minds. We could —"

"So here you are! I turn my back for an instant, and just look at the trouble you've gotten into!"

The authoritative voice — rather like the screech of a disturbed crow — caused Chase and Gypsy to step hurriedly apart, their expressions those of guilty children caught with their entire arms in a cookie jar. They turned toward the house, Gypsy with resignation and Chase with astonishment.

"Is *that* Amy?" he asked Gypsy in a comical aside.

"Uh-huh." Gypsy didn't dare look at Chase for fear of coming unglued. "Hi, Amy," she said in a stronger voice. "You turned your back for more than an instant, you turned it for *weeks.* Of course, I got into trouble." Chase poked her with an elbow, and she continued obediently, "Amy, this is Chase. The trouble I got into."

After a rather desperate look at Gypsy, Chase produced a winning smile. "Hello, Amy. It's nice to meet you finally, after —"

"You have a last name?" Amy demanded tersely, never one to possess scruples about interrupting other people in the middle of their sentences.

"Mitchell," Chase supplied in a failing voice.

Gypsy was coming unglued.

Amy was six feet tall in flat shoes (which she normally wore) and built like a fullback. She had long hair worn in a no-nonsense bun and as red as a fire engine, snapping blue eyes, and the kind of face artists drew on Vikings. That face had character; it also had the trick of looking like a scientist's face in the act of dispassionately studying the latest bug under a microscope.

She might have been any age between

forty-five and sixty-five, and looked about as capable as a human being could look without resembling a computer. She had no waist, and there was more of her going than coming, all of it tightly bound in gasping blue jeans and a peasant blouse. And her voice would easily wither a Bengal tiger in his tracks.

"So you're Mitchell. Rebecca told me about you." She looked Chase up and down with cold suspicion.

Recovering from that inspection — when Amy looked at you, he decided, your bones felt scoured — Chase hastily decided on a strategy. Exposure to Gypsy and her parents had taught him nothing if not that unpredictability was "a consummation devoutly to be wished." So he decided on a fast charge through forward enemy positions.

Stepping forward, he caught Amy around her nonexistent waist with both arms, planted a kiss squarely on her compressed lips, and said in a conspiratorial whisper, "You'll have to excuse us for a while, Amy; Gypsy and I are going to negotiate in a Jacuzzi."

He released her and turned to pick up a laughing Gypsy and toss her lightly over his shoulder. When he turned back, he saw that Amy's face had altered slightly. There was the faintest hint of a possibility that there *might* have been a twitch of her lips which an optimistic man would have called the beginnings of a smile.

"Negotiate what?" she asked. (Mildly for her, Chase decided, although a grizzly bear would have happily claimed it as a lethal growl.)

"Important things," Chase told her solemnly. "Like the number of children, and names for same . . . and cabbages and kings. You will excuse us?" he added politely.

"Certainly." Her voice was as polite as his, and her deadpan expression would have moved a marble statue to tears. "Supper's at seven — don't be late."

"We wouldn't think of it," Chase assured her, carrying his future bride over his shoulder and striding toward the deck at the rear of his house.

As he went up the steps to the deck Chase swatted a conveniently placed derriere, and said despairingly, "I was expecting a *motherly* sort of woman!"

"I know you were!" Gypsy was laughing so hard, she could barely speak. "Oh, God! Your expression was priceless!"

"Why didn't you warn me, you heartless little witch?" he demanded, setting her on her feet beside the Jacuzzi. The gleam in his eyes belied his fierce frown.

"And miss that little scene?" Gypsy choked. "I wish Poppy could have seen it; he'd have dined out on that for a month! Oh, darling, you were perfect — Amy loves you already."

"How could you tell?" Chase asked wryly, and then a sudden thought apparently occurred to him. "Gypsy . . . is Amy going to live with us?"

"Of course she is, darling," his future bride told him serenely.

Chase raised his eyes toward heaven with the look of a man whose cup was full. More than full. Running over.

"Don't worry." Gypsy patted his cheek gently. "If you're good, she'll only come after you with her broom once a week or so."

"Gypsy?"

"What is it, darling?"

"You're kidding?"

"No, darling."

"Gypsy?"

"Yes, darling?"

"I'll never survive it."

"Of course you will, darling." She smiled up at him sunnily. "My hero can adapt to anything. That's one of the reasons I love him."

"News for you, sweetheart," he murmured, kissing her nose. "Your hero has feet of clay."

Gypsy smiled very tenderly. "That's another of the reasons I love him."

"My Gypsy," he whispered. "My love."

They were late for supper. But Amy didn't fuss.

TEN

The shrill demand of the telephone finally roused Gypsy, and she felt a distinct inclination to swear sleepily. They'd flown half around the world the day before, from Geneva, Switzerland, to Portland, Oregon, with only brief layovers. Gypsy wasn't even sure what *month* it was — never mind the day. She was suffering from lack of sleep, a horrendous jet lag, and the irritating conviction that she'd forgotten *something* in Geneva.

And now the phone. It was only a little after eight a.m. — the birds weren't even up, for Pete's sake!

Gypsy half climbed over Chase to reach the phone; he was dead to the world and didn't move. She fumbled for the receiver and managed finally to lift it to her ear, murmuring, "What?"

"You've been gone," a soft, muffled masculine voice told her sadly. "For weeks . . .

and you didn't tell me. . . ."

Gypsy slammed the receiver down and sat bolt upright in bed, staring at the phone as if it had just this moment come to life. Now, *that* was a hell of a thing to wake up to in her condition! She had to ask Chase. She had to know.

Chase stirred and looked up at her with sleep-blurred eyes. "You look like a house fell on you," he observed, muffling a yawn with one hand. "Who was that on the phone?"

Shock tactics, she decided, might have some effect.

She snatched the sheet up to cover her breasts and stared at Chase in patent horror. "We have to get a divorce. Immediately," she announced in a very firm voice.

Chase raised himself on his elbow and stared at her with sleepy courtesy. "We just got *married* a few weeks ago," he pointed out patiently. "Are you tired of me already?"

Gypsy struggled hard to maintain her expression of shocked indignation. "I've married the wrong man! I fell in love with a voice over the telephone, and now I find out that it wasn't you at all. Get out of my bed!"

Chase was soothing. "You probably had a bad dream. Jet lag will do that to you. Lie

233

down, sweetheart."

"I want a divorce."

"I won't let you divorce me. I like being married. Besides, my father would stand me in front of a firing squad if I lost you. He's telling half of Geneva about his daughter-in-law, the famous writer."

"Well, if that's the only reason you want to hang on to me, I'll go and see a lawyer today!"

"It's Saturday."

"Is it? Monday, then."

Chase pulled her down beside him and arranged them both comfortably. "Not a chance. Amy loves me. And Corsair's coming around. You'd never find anyone as adaptable as me. Besides, we've already arranged to house-sit in Richmond for the winter."

With an inward sigh Gypsy abandoned her ploy to find out if Chase was really her "night lover." "Did we say hello to Jake and Sarah last night?" she asked suddenly. "I seem to remember something about it."

Chase laughed. "Well, sort of. I was carrying you, and you waved at them and asked how they liked my Jacuzzi. I think you were sound asleep at the time."

Gypsy frowned. "Were they over here,

then? Shouldn't they have been at your place?"

"Our place," Chase corrected. "And they were over here keeping Amy company until we arrived. Jake's determined to win her over," he added with a chuckle. "He says he wants the friendship of any woman who can defeat him at arm wrestling."

Gypsy accepted this information without a blink. "Oh." She yawned suddenly and changed the subject again. In an injured tone she said, "It's inhuman to drag a person halfway around the world. If man had been meant to fly —"

"He'd have wings?" Chase finished politely.

"No. He'd have a cushion tied to his rump to make up for airport lounges," she corrected disgustedly. "I seem to have spent eons in them, and my rump *hurts!*"

Chase patted it consolingly. "You'll recover. And, besides, whose fault was it that we made the trip in one fell swoop?"

"Mine, and don't rub it in." Gypsy sighed. "Can I help it if I wanted to get the whole thing over with as quickly as possible?"

"No, but you could have warned me before we went over that you had a phobia about flying."

"It isn't a phobia, it's just an uneasiness,"

she defended stoutly.

"Uh-huh." Chase grinned at her. "Tell me what the Swiss Alps look like from the air."

"I can't."

"Why not, sweetheart?"

"Because I had my eyes closed, and you know it, dammit!"

Chase laughed at her expression. "Seriously, honey, we should have taken Dad's suggestion: gone overland to Bordeaux and then taken a ship."

"Across the Atlantic?" Her tone was horrified.

They'd had this same discussion in Geneva, and Chase laughed as much now as he had then. "It beats me how you're willing to fly over an ocean, although you hate flying — but you aren't willing to sail across an ocean, although you love swimming."

"A plane's faster," Gypsy said definitely.

"So?"

"So don't make me explain my little irrational fears. I warned you long ago that I was no bargain, but you just wouldn't listen. So now you have an irrational wife."

"I have a wonderful wife," Chase corrected comfortably. "And I have Dad's stamp of approval to verify it. I thought he was going to cry when you hugged him that

236

last time at the airport. You definitely made a conquest there."

Gypsy smiled. "I love your dad. He reminds me of Poppy — very quiet, but with a deadly sense of humor."

"Mmmm. I think you've about got him talked into settling in Portland when he retires. You can work on him some more when he comes over for Christmas."

"It'd be nice to have both families nearby," she agreed, then frowned as part of his remark set up a train of thought. "Christmas. That reminds me — before we left for Geneva, I saw you and Mother come in here with a package all wrapped up. It looked like a painting. Somehow or another, I forgot to ask you about it."

Chase laughed silently. "That's my Gypsy — give her enough time, and she'll get around to it eventually!"

Gypsy raised up on an elbow and stared down at him severely. "Stop avoiding the subject. What have you and my mother been up to?"

"That question sounds vaguely indecent," he murmured.

"Chase!"

"I have a shrewish wife," he told the ceiling, then relented as the gleam in her eyes threatened grievous bodily harm. "Take a look behind you, shrew," he invited. "On the wall — where you were too much asleep last night to notice it."

Gypsy twisted around to look. Then she sat up and looked a while longer. Then she looked at Chase as he sat up beside her.

He smiled. "Rebecca painted it for me. Although she said she didn't know why I wanted it — since I was bound to end up with the original. I asked her to paint it that Sunday I invited them for lunch. And we left it here because I knew we'd spend our first night back in this room."

After a moment he added softly, "I didn't know she'd put me in it."

Gypsy looked at the painting again. Her first thought was that Rebecca must have seen the seascapes in Chase's bedroom and, with her usual perception, decided to paint another seascape which would blend in . . . and yet stand out. Because this painting wasn't bleak or lonely.

The central figure was Gypsy. She was wearing the silk nightgown and leaning back against the rock jutting up behind her, staring out to sea. Above her were storm clouds, curiously shaped, as if Nature had been in a teasing mood that day, bent on luring mortals out to sea. The clouds were wispy, insubstantial; their dreamy visions seen only

238

by those who cared to see. There was a unicorn leaping from one cloud, a castle topped another; a rainbow cast its hazy colors over the ghost-ship sailing beneath it, a ghostly pirate at its wheel. There was Apollo, driving his sun behind dark clouds; there was a masked figure on a white steed; there was a knight climbing toward his cloud-castle.

And there was Chase — real, substantial. The view caught him from the waist up, half hidden by the rock Gypsy was leaning against. And Chase wasn't looking out to sea at the siren-visions of clouds. He was looking at Gypsy, and his face was soft with yearning.

Gypsy took a deep breath, realizing only then that she'd suspended breathing for what seemed like eternal seconds. "I never stop wondering at Mother's perception," she murmured almost inaudibly. She looked again at the cloud-heroes, seeing in each one an elusive resemblance to Chase.

"She saw it, Chase — she saw it all. I was looking at visions of heroes and seeing you without realizing it."

"And I was looking at you," Chase murmured, bending his head to kiss her bare shoulder.

"I'm so glad you're a patient hero," she

239

whispered, smiling up at him as he lowered them both back to the comfortable pillows.

Chase grinned faintly. "An original hero, anyway. What other man would have scoured Geneva — of all places! — to find a Buddha with a clock in his middle?"

Gypsy giggled helplessly. "Did you see your dad's face when we carried it in? And when you told him very seriously that your watch had stopped?"

"He looked even more peculiar when we opened the other boxes," Chase noted ruefully. "Such odd souvenirs for a honeymoon: an abstract wooden sculpture of a knight on horseback, a bogus nineteenth-century sword — complete with scabbard, a hideous little genie-type lamp covered with tarnish. . . . You'd do great on a scavenger hunt, sweetheart."

"*You're* the one who fell in love with the sword," Gypsy pointed out calmly.

"A memento of our courtship," Chase said soulfully.

"Right. Just don't try to dance while wearing it."

"As long as you don't try to conjure a genie from that lamp."

"Why not?" she asked in mock disappointment.

"I shudder to think what'd pop out."

Gypsy sighed. "You're probably right."

"And speaking of being right" — he patted her gently — "I've been meaning to tell you that the Swiss cooking did wonders in adding that extra ballast you needed."

"Uh-huh." Gypsy twisted slightly for a view of her blanket-covered posterior. "Too much ballast, if you ask me. Just look! I'm getting broad in the beam!"

He choked on a laugh. "Your beam looks great to me."

"Flatterer."

"The choice of words was yours." He drew her a bit closer. "Besides, you still weigh no more than a midget. I'll have to fatten you up some more before we go to work on Radinka or Shadwell."

Gypsy started laughing. "You're hung up on those names! I thought you just used them as a terrifying example of the names I'd come up with on my own."

Sheepishly Chase murmured, "They kinda grow on you though."

"No, Chase," she told him firmly.

"I suppose not. Still —"

"No."

"No?"

"Definitely no. I'd be a widow as soon as the kids realized what you'd done to them."

He sighed. "My first opportunity to come

up with some really creative names," he mourned sadly.

"Exercise your creative powers by naming Angel's kittens. Or you can name the Mercedes. Or we'll get a dog —"

"We already have one," Chase told her casually.

Gypsy lifted her head to stare down at him. "We do?"

"Uh-huh. Bucephalus."

"But he belongs to the Robbinses —"

"Not anymore. Remember when we called before the wedding to explain about Amy being in sole charge of the house while we were gone?" When Gypsy nodded, he went on. "You had to leave the room because Rebecca wanted to talk to you about flowers or something. Anyway, I was talking to Tim. It seems he's been offered a two-year position, which could turn out to be permanent, in London starting next year. Bucephalus would have to spend six months in quarantine, and he'd be miserable. So Tim offered to give him to us. I accepted — for both of us."

Gypsy smiled. "That's wonderful. Now we have a head start on our family."

Chase began to nuzzle her throat. "Mmmm. Would you care to start working toward the rest of our family, Gypsy mine?"

"I thought you'd never ask," she murmured, feeling that delicious tremor stir to life inside her. Then she smiled, and said almost to herself, "Gypsy mine; you've called me that from the first. Were you that sure of me, darling?"

"Not sure. Hopeful." Chase pulled her easily over on top of him and smiled up at her whimsically. "I've never been one to search for rainbows, but you were my dream." He hesitated, then added very softly, " 'So if I dream I have you, I have you.' "

A thousand and one thoughts tumbled through Gypsy's mind.

"What is it, love?" Chase asked gently. "You're giving me a very peculiar look."

Gypsy carefully searched her memory of events. She was almost sure — Yes, she *was* sure! Her "night lover" had called only twice when Chase was actually in the room, and on both occasions, she'd hung up on him before he could say more than a few words. What if . . . what if she *hadn't* been so quick to hang up? Would she have discovered that it had been a tape-recorded message? Held up to the phone by a helpful friend, perhaps?

"You're staring at me, love. Somewhat fiercely, I might add."

"Chase . . ."

"Yes, love?"

"You just quoted Donne."

"Did I, love?" He was smiling slightly, the jade eyes veiled by sleepy lids. "The man obviously had a way with words."

"Chase."

"Hmmm?"

"It was you. It *was* you . . . wasn't it?"

"What was me, love?"

Gypsy tried to ignore wandering hands. "The phone calls. It had to be you. Wasn't it you?"

"I don't know what you're talking about, love."

"Chase, you *have* to tell me! I'll go nuts, and —" A startled giggle suddenly escaped her.

Jade eyes gleamed up at her, filled with laughter. "Ah-ha! I finally found your ticklish spot. You're at my mercy now, love."

Gypsy choked back another giggle, trying to ward off his tickling hand. "Chase! Stop that! And tell me it was you, dammit! Darling, I have to *know!*"

"What was that, love? Didn't quite catch it."

"Chase!" she wailed.

He smiled.

ABOUT THE AUTHOR

Kay Hooper is the award-winning author of *Hunting Fear, Chill of Fear, Touching Evil, Whisper of Evil, Sense of Evil, Once a Thief, Always a Thief,* the Shadows trilogy, and other novels. She lives in North Carolina. Her next book, *Blood Dreams,* is coming soon from Bantam.